Praise for the Tj Jensen Mystery Series

"Daley's characters come to life on the page. Her novels are filled with a little mystery and a little romance which makes for a murderous adventure."

– Tonya Kappes,
USA Today Bestselling Author of *Fixin' To Die*

"Daley's mysteries offer as much sizzle and pop as fireworks on a hot summer's day."

– Mary Kennedy,
Author of The Dream Club Mysteries

"I'm a huge fan of Kathi's books. I think I've read every one. Without a doubt, she's a gifted cozy mystery author and I eagerly await each new release!"

– Dianne Harman,
Author of the High Desert Cozy Mysteries

"Intriguing, likeable characters, keep-you-guessing mysteries, and settings that literally transport you to Paradise...Daley's stories draw you in and keep you glued until the very last page."

– Tracy Weber,
Agatha-Nominated Author of the Downward Dog Mysteries

"Daley really knows how to write a top-notch cozy."

– *MJB Reviewers*

"Kathi Daley writes a story with a puzzling cold-case mystery while highlighting...the love of home, family, and good friends."

– *Chatting About Cozies*

Treasure in Paradise

The Tj Jensen Mystery Series
by Kathi Daley

PUMPKINS IN PARADISE (#1)
SNOWMEN IN PARADISE (#2)
BIKINIS IN PARADISE (#3)
CHRISTMAS IN PARADISE (#4)
PUPPIES IN PARADISE (#5)
HALLOWEEN IN PARADISE (#6)
TREASURE IN PARADISE (#7)
FIREWORKS IN PARADISE (#8)

Treasure in Paradise

A TJ Jensen Mystery

KATHI DALEY

HENERY PRESS

TREASURE IN PARADISE
A Tj Jensen Mystery
Part of the Henery Press Mystery Collection

First Edition | April 2017

Henery Press, LLC
www.henerypress.com

This is a work of fiction. Any references to historical events, real people, or real locales are used fictitiously. Other names, characters, places, and incidents are the product of the author's imagination, and any resemblance to actual events or locales or persons, living or dead, is entirely coincidental.

Trade Paperback ISBN-13: 978-1-63511-191-0
Digital epub ISBN-13: 978-1-63511-192-7
Kindle ISBN-13: 978-1-63511-193-4
Hardcover Paperback ISBN-13: 978-1-63511-194-1

Printed in the United States of America

This book is dedicated to my father, Mike Dooley,
for teaching me the value of hard work, commitment,
and dedication to my goals.

ACKNOWLEDGMENTS

They say it takes a village, and I have a great one.

I want to thank all my friends who hang out over at my Kathi Daley Books Group page on Facebook. This exceptional group help me not only with promotion but with helpful suggestion and feedback as well.

I want to thank the bloggers who have pretty much adopted me and have helped me to build a fantastic social media presence. There are too many to list, but I want to specifically recognize Lori Caswell and Great Escape Tours for putting together the most awesome launch tours ever.

I want to thank my fellow authors who I run to all the time when I don't know how to do something or how to deal with a situation. I have to say that the cozy mystery family is about as close knit a family as you are likely to find anywhere.

I want to thank Bruce Curran for generously helping me with all my techy questions, Ricky Turner for help with my webpage, and Peggy Hyndman for help sleuthing out those pesky typos.

I want to thank my graphic designer, Jessica Fisher, for all my flashy ads and headers.

I want to thank Randy Ladenheim-Gil for making what I write legible.

I want to thank Art Molinares for welcoming me so enthusiastically to the Henery Press family, and a special thank you to Erin George and the entire editing crew who have been so incredibly awesome and fun to work with.

And last, but certainly not least, I want to thank my super-husband, Ken, for allowing me time to write by taking care of everything else (and I mean everything).

CHAPTER 1

Friday, June 16

There is magic in beginnings. Some beginnings come as a rite of passage, such as a graduation from college, the birth of a child, or a wedding day. Other beginnings start off more subtly, as nothing more than an ordinary moment that evolves into a crucial event that, in the end, helps define who you are and who you will become.

And then there are the beginnings that arrive on the heels of change. At times we welcome this change with joyful anticipation, while other times we fight to maintain that which we feel we've lost. Change can come in gentle waves that shepherd us into a new reality, or it can come in a tornado of destruction that tears apart everything we hold dear to our hearts.

My own new beginning occurred when I packed up two sisters, a grandpa, two very dear friends, four cats, and three dogs and traveled across the country to help an old friend of my father's renovate the oceanfront resort he'd been forced to sell. The Turtle Cove Resort, which consisted of a resident's home and twenty cabins nestled artfully on a long stretch of beach on the southeastern corner of Gull Island, had been in Garrett Hanford's family for four generations. Garrett was an only child who'd never married or had children of his own, so when his health began to fail he'd decided he had no choice other than to sell the property he was no longer capable of managing.

The problem was that the resort had fallen into disrepair, and the only buyers interested in the large slice of oceanfront land were developers who didn't care about the cabins because they planned to tear them down and build a new infrastructure from the ground up. Garrett didn't want to sell to those large corporations, so in spite of the fact that he wasn't likely to recover his investment, he'd decided to put some money into the resort and renovate the buildings prior to looking for a buyer who would maintain the integrity of the property he loved. When I learned Garrett had suffered a stroke and would need someone to oversee the renovations, I jumped at the chance to take a step away from a life that had undergone so many changes in the past few months that I no longer recognized it. What I didn't expect was that by agreeing to spend the summer on Gull Island, I would be trading one set of problems for another.

"Someone from the sheriff's office should be here in a few minutes," my best friend, Kyle Donovan, informed me as he joined me in the attic of the three-story house where the two of us, along with my two half-sisters Ashley and Gracie, my Grandpa Ben, and a dear friend, Stan Griffin, planned to live that summer.

I put my hand over my nose to help ward off the stench as I glanced at the partially decomposed body in the middle of the room. "What do you think happened to him?"

Kyle's sandy blond hair had grown long over the past few months and touched his collar when he shrugged. "I'm sure the deputy who shows up will be able to tell us. It looks like he's been dead for a while."

"Two weeks at least," Stan, more commonly known as Doc, agreed. Doc was not only my grandfather, Ben Jensen's, best friend but also a retired coroner, so he knew what he was talking about. "I can't say for certain without a closer examination of the remains, but based on the fractures on the man's left temple, I'm going to say the cause of death was blunt force trauma delivered by a right-handed individual facing him."

I grimaced. I didn't know exactly what I expected to find on my first day in over twenty years at Turtle Cove Resort, but in spite of my reputation for having a nose for mysteries, I certainly didn't think I'd be thrust into a murder investigation before I'd even had a chance to unpack.

"Are you okay, Tj?" Kyle asked as Doc slipped on the latex gloves he carried in his wallet and took a closer look at the body.

"I'm fine now that my heart has stopped pounding." I looked around the dusty room. "It's been such a long time since I was here, but everything looks exactly like I remember."

"You spent a lot of time in the attic as a kid?"

"Actually, I did."

Kyle frowned.

"It's not like it sounds." I laid my head on Kyle's shoulder as I silently gave thanks for the friend who'd not only helped me through the past couple of months, but who had willingly and enthusiastically given up his own life to follow me across the country for the summer. "Garrett didn't abuse me or anything. In fact, he was very nice to me despite the fact I was pretty horrible to him."

Kyle wrapped his arm around my shoulder. "I can't imagine you being horrible to anyone."

"Believe it. It was the summer after my grandmother passed away. My dad had a conference that he had to attend in

Charleston and he didn't want to leave me home alone with my grandpa since he already had his hands full running the resort. Normally my grandmother took charge of me when my dad was away, but after her passing Dad decided to bring me with him to Gull Island. I stayed with Garrett during the day while my dad went to meetings, although he did come back to the island each night. I was mad that I had to come on the trip when I really wanted to stay home, so I'm afraid I went out of my way to make everyone's life miserable. Partly by sequestering myself in the attic and refusing to participate in any of the fun Garrett had planned for me."

"I guess I see where Ashley get her angsty nature," Kyle teased.

"Very funny," I shot back, although I supposed Kyle had a point. I had behaved as badly the summer I'd spent on Gull Island as my sister Ashely had been since we'd left Paradise Lake. "Shouldn't the deputy be here by now?"

"It's hasn't been that long and it's not like this is an emergency," Kyle answered. "The man has been dead for quite some time, so a few more minutes won't matter."

"I wonder who he is."

"Buck Barnes," Doc said from behind us.

I turned and looked at Doc, who had completed his investigation and was standing over the body.

"You know him?"

"No. He had a business card in his shirt pocket."

"Business card? What sort of business was he in?"

"Treasure hunting."

Okay, that got my attention. "Treasure hunting, as in buried treasure?"

Doc shrugged. "I suppose. The card is the type printed on a computer. It simply has the man's name printed under the words 'treasure hunter.' There's a photo at the top and a small treasure chest in the corner, but that's it. The card doesn't even have a phone number or address."

"I wonder what a treasure hunter would be doing in Garrett's attic." I looked around the large room that was cluttered with discarded objects from generations past. It was obvious someone had been looking for something specific. Boxes had been upended to reveal the treasures that most likely only held value for the person who had stored them here.

"From where I'm standing, it looks like a lot of junk," Kyle said, mirroring my own thoughts. "Discarded clothing, old photo albums, an abandoned cane, various knickknacks that would only have sentimental value. I suppose there could have been something of value that was found and removed by whoever killed the treasure hunter."

I was about to respond when I heard a sound behind me. I turned to find a tall man with short dark hair dressed in a brown uniform standing in the doorway that led to the staircase. He frowned as he looked around the room, which had obviously been ransacked.

"My name is Deputy Savage. Are you Tj Jensen?"

"I am," I said.

"I see you solved the mystery of where Buck Barnes has been for the past eighteen days."

"Eighteen days? Garrett had his stroke almost six weeks ago. Any idea what Buck Barnes was doing up here when Garrett wasn't even on the island?"

Deputy Savage seemed to ignore my question as he bent down to take a closer look at the body. He pulled on gloves before carefully turning the head to one side. He must have been satisfied, or perhaps dissatisfied, by what he found, because he stood back up, tugged off his gloves, and looked directly at me. "When exactly did you arrive on the island?"

"Just a couple of hours ago. When we arrived at the Turtle

Cove Resort we realized the front door had been left unlocked. Garrett had specifically told me that he'd locked the place up before he left, so we suspected there might have been a break-in. Kyle and I decided to take a look around while Doc and my grandpa helped my sisters unload the animals. When we came upstairs we found the body. Kyle asked Doc to come up and then he called you right away."

The deputy looked at Doc. "You're a doctor?"

"Retired coroner."

"I see." The man turned back to me. "Where are your sisters and your grandfather now?"

"Walking the dogs."

Deputy Savage made a couple of notes on the clipboard he carried. "I'll need to verify with Garrett that you're authorized to be here, but given you have a key I'll take your word for it for the time being."

"Thank you. I have a number for the rehab facility Garrett was moved to. I can get it if you'd like."

"I'll get it before I leave. For now, I just need to see some ID."

Doc had warned us that the representative from the sheriff's office would want that, so we were all prepared, although I'd have rather walked on fire than show the photo on my driver's license to *anyone*. My hair appeared more red than auburn and more frizzy than curly, and rather than a welcoming smile there were lips peeled back in such a way as to provide the image of a woman who looked like she was on the verge of a very unladylike sneeze.

The deputy chuckled but didn't comment. "It says you live in Nevada?"

"I do. We all do."

"What brought you to our island?"

Now that, I realized, was a loaded question. In order to

understand why I would pack up, in addition to myself, five people and seven animals and drive almost three thousand miles for a summer job that didn't really pay anything, you have to understand the upheaval my life had gone through during the past couple of months, but that, I was afraid, was a story for another day.

I looked at the deputy, who was waiting for my answer. "Garrett Hanford is a friend of my father. He needed someone to oversee the renovations he's planning for the resort, so I volunteered to stay here for the summer."

"And the others?"

"Friends and family who volunteered to help out."

"I heard Garrett was going to sell to one of those developers who've been hounding him for almost a decade. The man I spoke to told me he plans to tear everything down and start over, so why is he renovating?"

"He doesn't want to sell to the developer," I answered. "He plans to fix the place up and then look for a buyer who will leave the resort intact."

Deputy Savage raised an eyebrow before jotting something else down on his clipboard.

"Do you think that's important?" I asked.

"It might be."

"Do you care to elaborate?"

"No."

I guess I couldn't blame the guy. I wasn't a cop and I hadn't known Savage my whole life, like I knew the deputy back home. He had no reason to share what he knew with me, but I had an inquiring mind and I'd grown used to being kept in the loop, which simply meant if Savage wouldn't share, I'd have to do some snooping and figure it out for myself.

Deputy Savage walked around the room, making notes on his clipboard, while Doc, Kyle, and I stood off to the side. He asked a few additional questions as he worked, but mostly he just jotted down notes as he inspected the room. I wasn't sure what he was looking for, or whether or not he found it, but I did notice him frown just prior to the arrival of a giant bird that flew in through the open window, causing me to jump into the air as I let out a startled scream.

"Man overboard, man overboard," the bird, which I realized was a colorful parrot, repeated.

"There you are, you shifty bird," Savage growled at the newcomer. "I've had half the island looking for you."

"This is your bird?" I asked.

"Garrett's. After he had his stroke I came by to get the bird, but he managed to escape when I tried to transfer him into a carrier. I've been trying to catch the slippery impersonator ever since. He's been seen around town, but no one has been able to snag him."

"Garrett didn't mention that his bird was missing."

"He doesn't know. I figured he had enough to worry about without wondering if Blackbeard was okay. As far as Garrett knows, the bird has been staying with the local vet since he's been away." Savage looked at Kyle, who was closest to the window. "Close the window real quietlike before the sneaky beast flies back out."

Kyle did as he was asked, but I had the feeling the bird was quite happy to find people in his house. He'd perched atop the highest bookshelf and watched us as we talked.

"What did he mean by man overboard?" I wondered.

"He's a bird. I doubt he meant anything," Savage pointed out.

Deputy Savage walked across the room and knelt down next to a box which had been upended. He righted the box before picking up a discarded cane. He turned it over in his hands several times before setting it aside. He stood up, turned, and looked at me. "Garrett kept treats for Blackbeard in the storage area beneath the cage in the sunroom. Why don't you take the bird downstairs and get him settled? Just be sure the door is closed. I don't want him getting out again." Savage looked toward where Kyle and Doc were standing. "I need to look around a bit, if you don't mind waiting for me downstairs as well."

The three of us, along with Blackbeard, headed downstairs to wait. When Blackbeard saw his cage, he flew in through the open door and settled on his perch.

"Close the door, close the door."

I did as Blackbeard instructed. It appeared he was happy to be home. I gave the colorful bird one of the cookies the deputy had told me about and turned back toward Kyle, who was grinning at the turn of events.

"Looks like we can add a bird to our menagerie."

"Looks like," I agreed. "We'll have to keep an eye on the cats. As long as Blackbeard is in the cage he should be safe, but we'll need to watch him if we let him out. It sounds like there's a car in the drive."

Kyle and I returned to the front of the house, where Doc was speaking to a man who identified himself as working for the local mortuary. Doc showed him to the stairway that led to the attic and then rejoined Kyle and me.

Once Buck's body had been removed and Deputy Savage had gone, my entourage and I set to making our temporary house into a home while avoiding the attic completely. Doc, Kyle, and Grandpa began to unload the moving van we'd hired while my sisters, Ashley and Gracie, each picked out a bedroom. I decided it was best to call Garrett to let him know what was going on before he heard about it from anyone else.

It was a beautiful day. The sun was shining and the air temperature hovered in the mid-eighties. I grabbed a diet soda from the ice chest we'd used for the trip east and headed out onto the deck behind the house, which overlooked a sandy beach and the deep blue sea. As I dialed the phone I braced myself for Garrett's reaction. I expected him to be saddened by what had occurred, but instead of grief, the emotion I picked up on was anger.

"Dammit. I told Buck that his incessant hunt for the treasure was going to get him killed. The man had a head as thick as his waistline."

"Treasure?"

"Barkley's Treasure. Remember, I told you about it when you visited that summer."

I thought back to my time on the island and tried to remember what Garrett and I had talked about. "The man in the café in town," I remembered. "He interrupted our lunch to ask you about a map. I wondered what map and you told me a story about a pirate and his treasure. I thought the story was a fairytale. It was real?"

"My dad seemed to think it was real, but there are others who agree with the fairytale theory. The legend of Barkley's treasure has been around for more than a century, and while many have searched for it, as far as I know, no one has found it, but that doesn't mean it isn't real."

"So you think Buck was in your attic looking for treasure?"

"I think he was in the attic looking for a map. Chances are he shot off his mouth about the dang thing and someone followed him to the house."

"So there actually is a map hidden in your attic?"

"Not anymore. My mother destroyed it after my dad died."

"Why would your mom destroy a map that was supposed to lead to a treasure?"

"She blamed the map for both my grandfather's and my father's deaths. Some think that she acted rashly, but I don't blame her for doing what she did. I've seen what greed can do to a person. I tried to tell Buck that the map was long gone, but he thought I was holding out on him."

"So there's no map to find."

"'Fraid not."

I realized something wasn't adding up. I thought the resort had been in Garrett's family for four generations, but based on what he'd just told me it didn't sound like the men from whom he'd descended had devoted much time to building and running a resort. "If your grandfather and father were treasure hunters, who did you inherit the resort from?"

"My mother, God rest her soul. Unlike my father, who was a dreamer, my mother was a pragmatist. She worked hard to make the resort her father left her profitable while raising me on her own. The resort meant a lot to her, and it means a lot to me. Thank you again for agreeing to oversee the renovations and the sale of the property. I won't be able to rest until I know the property is in the hands of someone who will maintain the integrity of the lifestyle my family worked so hard to create."

"It really is a great property, and I agree it would be a shame to tear down the house and cabins to build a high-rise."

"It would be more than just a shame; it would be a tragedy. Do you know that we have turtles that return to the beach just beyond cabin twelve to nest every year? And the marsh to the west of the property is home to a huge variety of birds and other wildlife that depend on a pristine environment to thrive. There are plenty of islands in the area that cater to people looking for the megaresort experience, but Gull Island has always been a place to escape the insanity of modern-day life and take a step back in time."

I could tell that Garrett was passionate about his desire to protect the integrity of the land he'd inherited and found I agreed with him. Allowing a developer to come in and build a megaresort would ruin the personality of Gull Island.

"Don't worry. I'll find you the perfect buyer," I promised.

"You should talk to Meg over at the museum. She also runs the local turtle rescue organization. She can provide you with the education you need to take over as the guardian of the turtles who nest on Turtle Beach while you're occupying the property."

"I'll do that."

"Meg is really something. She'll talk your ear off, but you won't find a finer woman anywhere. Saving the turtles is a popular movement on the island. Chances are you'll run into a chap by the name of Digger on the beach. He's very active in the rescue movement. Some would say too active."

"What do you mean?"

"He tends to take his mission to protect the turtles and the eggs to the next level. Been known to run people off with a pellet gun if he finds them disturbing the nests."

"If I run into him, I'll tread lightly," I promised.

I paused and listened as Garrett spoke to someone in the background regarding his physical therapy. Kyle walked into the room with Blackbeard on his shoulder while I waited for Garrett to return to the conversation. "Playing pirate?"

Kyle laughed. "Maybe."

"Pirate's treasure, pirate's treasure."

"Is that Blackbeard?" Garrett came back on the line.

"Yeah. He's playing pirate with my friend Kyle."

Garrett chuckled. "That's his favorite game, but I thought he was at the veterinarian's."

I thought quickly. "He was, but he was homesick, so we decided it was best for him to stay here until you're recovered enough to have him with you."

"I'm really happy to hear that. I sure do miss the big guy."

"I'm sure he misses you as well. Have you had any news on when you might be able to return to Gull Island?"

"The doctors aren't saying, which is frustrating. Everyone keeps reminding me that I've had a serious setback and need to be patient, but between you and me I'm done being patient."

"Hang in there. I'm sure everyone just wants to make sure that you take the time you need."

"I guess. As much as I am enjoying chatting with you, the nurse is motioning me to hang up. I'm not a fan of the therapy they have me doing, but I've found resisting doesn't get me anywhere, so I suppose I should say goodbye."

"If you want to regain your mobility you need to do what the therapist tells you."

"Yes, Mother. Feel free to call again with any questions you might have about the property."

"I will. And Garrett, take care. I really would like to see you back to your old self."

I hung up, and Kyle moved Blackbeard's cage into the living room, where he could be around the family, while I headed upstairs to see if everyone was getting settled in. The resident's house was a large structure that at one time had been used as a lodge. There were ten bedrooms, seven bathrooms, a large common room, a huge kitchen, and a roomy dining area. The girls had picked out a room for me at the back of the house overlooking the beach. It was by far the nicest room in the house, and I was touched they'd saved it for me and one of them hadn't claimed it. Ashley had taken a room at the end of the hall, and Gracie took the room between the two of us. Both Doc and Grandpa Ben had chosen rooms at the front of the house, and Kyle had decided to bunk in the bedroom off the kitchen downstairs.

"I guess we should have stopped at the grocery store on our

way out here," Kyle commented after he'd returned Blackbeard to his cage and joined me.

"I didn't want the animals to have to wait in the car. Once we get them settled we can head into town for a bite to eat. I remember there being a diner on the pier that had fabulous food. It was owned by one of the nicest women I've ever met. I'm not sure she's still on the island, but we need to eat and the view is spectacular."

"Sounds like a good plan. If you want to make me a grocery list, we can take two cars into town and I'll stop to pick up some essentials after we eat while you finish getting everyone settled."

"What about the van rental? We'll need to return it to the dealer in Charleston. I guess I can follow you over with the car."

"We'll take care of that in a day or two. Maybe even next week some time. Let's get everyone settled in first. I have a feeling that both the kids and the animals will be able to begin to relax once we establish some sort of a regular routine."

"Speaking of the animals, have you seen the cats?"

"I locked them in one of the bedrooms upstairs until we get everything unpacked. I didn't want them getting out."

"Good idea. We'll need to be sure the girls understand that we need to keep the door to Blackbeard's cage closed to protect him from the resident felines."

"I already had a talk with them about that very thing," Kyle assured me. "What did Garrett have to say?"

"He thinks Buck was in the attic looking for a map Garrett claims his mother destroyed years ago after his father died looking for some treasure. According to Garrett, that treasure seems to have invited any number of dreamers to the island, all of them certain they have what it takes to find long-lost gold. It's Garrett's opinion that Buck told someone about the map, and that *someone* followed him to the house and killed him."

"If the map was destroyed, we know the person who killed

Barnes didn't find it. Do you think they'll come back around looking for it?"

"I suppose it's possible, but they'd have to get past three dogs and four cats."

Kyle laughed. "In spite of our intimidating menagerie I think I'll have an alarm installed. As far as I'm concerned, the real treasure is the people living in the house and I want to be certain everyone is safe."

CHAPTER 2

I'd fallen in love with Gertie Newsome, owner of Gertie's on the Wharf, the moment I met her when I'd visited as a child. The free spirit with a long gray braid that hung down the back of her bright pink peasant top was a large woman with an equally large personality. She was loud and opinionated and reminded me a lot of Doc, who was one of the most gregarious people I had ever met.

"Come on over here and give me some sugar." Gertie wrapped me in a bear hug that, due to her ample bosom and my petite stature, threatened to suffocate me. "Garrett told me you were coming to the island for the summer." Gertie pushed me away slightly. "Just look at you. Ain't you a sight for sore eyes?"

"I've missed you too." I smiled at her. She was one of the few people I remembered meeting during my time on the island.

"Are these here your youngins?"

I took a step back. "This is Ashley and Gracie. They're actually my half-sisters, but I've been their guardian since my mom died."

"Come on over here and give Auntie Gertie a hug." Gertie opened her arms and enveloped both sisters. Gracie, who was eight, seemed to be thrilled with the attention of the unreserved woman, but Ashley, who was eleven and much less comfortable with public displays of affection, looked like she wanted to kick her. I quickly ushered the girls into a booth while Gertie greeted Kyle.

"You certainly have a great location out here on the wharf," Kyle politely commented as he quickly slid into the booth, I imagined, to avoid his own bear hug.

"Best spot on the island. Best food too. I bet you're a fish-and-chips kind of guy. I made them fresh with fish caught this morning."

"Sounds good," Kyle replied.

"And you." Gertie smiled at Doc as she placed a hand on his shoulder. "What a fine specimen of a man. Strong and ample. I bet you're a beef eater. I have a prime rib sandwich with coleslaw that will stick to your ribs."

I was pretty sure Doc actually blushed as he agreed that he would indeed be interested in the dinner option Gertie had suggested.

Gertie correctly guessed that Grandpa would like the meatloaf, the girls would like grilled cheeses with fries, and I'd like a seafood salad. When she nailed the drink orders as well I was convinced she was some sort of food psychic.

I looked around the room while Gertie assembled our drinks and sent our order to the kitchen. The interior of the café was tastefully decorated with bleached fishing nets hung on walls adorned with items from the sea. The walls were painted a light blue that accentuated the white of the nets and brought a feeling of lightness to the open and airy room. There were windows along three of the walls that looked out over the harbor, which was dotted with colorful boats bobbing to and fro on the gentle waves. The exterior of the building had been set up to accommodate outdoor dining, currently closed due to routine maintenance before the busy summer season kicked off.

"Can I go watch the boats come in?" Gracie asked.

I looked out the window. It didn't appear that going out onto the deck would be a problem in spite of the fact that it wasn't set up to serve food.

"I'll go with her," Kyle offered.

"I want to come," Ashley joined in.

"Okay, but only for a few minutes. I'm sure it won't take too long for us to get our food."

Doc decided to go with Kyle and the girls and Grandpa announced his intention to go wash up, which left me sitting alone at the table.

"Heard about Buck," Gertie said after delivering our drinks. "Such a damn shame."

"That was fast."

"Island gossip hotline. It's faster and more dependable than the nightly news."

"I see. I guess that's a reliable perk of small-town life. We have a similar network back home in Serenity, but I'm not sure it's quite as fast as your network."

"News doesn't always travel quite that fast, but the woman who answers the phone for the sheriff is a friend of mine. She called me two minutes after you called her to let me know that you'd found a body in the attic. I didn't find out that it was Buck until after Deputy Savage returned to the office."

"I guess the news must have come as quite a shock."

"Not really. Everyone knew that treasure was going to get Buck killed. He was a nice guy. It really is a damn shame everyone was right."

"Did you know him well?"

Gertie tilted her head as if considering my question. "Buck was one of those sweet old guys who was born and raised on the island but never did amount to anything. He was as nice as nice can be, but he wasn't carrying a full deck, if you know what I mean. The proprietors in the area sort of adopted him. He never could hold down a job, but we all looked out for him, paying him to sweep up and do other odd jobs."

"That's really nice."

"You know that those of us who make the island our home are like a family."

I did remember that in spite of the angst I harbored the summer of my visit, those I did let in were some of the nicest people I'd ever met.

"You mentioned that the treasure was most likely responsible for Barnes's death, but it looked to me like someone killed him."

Normally I wouldn't bring up this particular subject in a dining establishment, but it was an off time of day—late for lunch and early for dinner—so, other than whoever was in the kitchen, Gertie and I were the only ones there.

"Buck was an outgoing sort who would more likely than not strike up a conversation with anyone he happened across in the course of his day. While that's something those of us who knew him well loved about him, he did have a tendency to attract attention from certain individuals he was better off not fraternizing with."

"Like who?"

"Like tourists who came to the island chasing after the same legend Buck devoted his life to. He had an arsenal of stories at his disposal, some true but most made up. He'd get to sharing his experiences with total strangers who caught the fever after hearing one of Buck's elaborate tales."

"And no one tried to stop him from talking?"

"We did. But Buck was a stubborn one, and to be honest, the treasure hunters who visit this area make up a significant percentage of our annual tourism. I guess none of us wanted to squelch Buck's enthusiasm completely."

"Can you think of anyone specific who seemed like they could be a threat to Buck?"

Gertie paused. "You thinking of digging around in this?"

"No, not at all. I'm just curious."

"Uh-huh." Gertie looked at me doubtfully. "Your daddy was in last summer when he was on the island visiting Garrett. We shared a spot of moonshine while we caught up. He told me that you'd turned into some sort of an amateur detective. Seems like a mysterious death your first day on the island would be something you PI types would be interested in following up on."

"I'm not a private investigator and I'm not a detective. At least not officially. I do have a very active curiosity, and it does seem that I tend to get pulled into whatever seems to be going on at the moment."

"I'm not surprised a bit." Gertie chuckled as she slid onto the bench across from me. "I knew you had the eye when I met you as a child."

"The eye?"

"Sort of like a sixth sense that tells you what to notice and what not to bother yourself with. My granny had the gift. Always knew what was gonna happen before it happened, and then once it did happen she'd know just what to look for to help explain things. You know, the first time you met me you asked about my black cat. Now the fact that a young girl would ask about a cat isn't all that odd, but the thing is I had just gotten the cat and no one, including Garrett, even knew I had it. When I asked you how you knew, you pointed out a single piece of cat hair on my blouse. Like I said. You had the eye."

I smiled. I doubted I had this supernatural power that Gertie seemed to be alluding to, and noticing cat hair on a person's blouse didn't seem like it was any sort of superpower, but suddenly I remembered exactly what I'd loved about the jolly woman from the diner.

"I forgot how much I missed you after I returned home from my trip that summer. Do you still believe in ghosts?"

"Be a damn fool not to."

"One still living in your house?"

"Goin' on thirty years now. I know there are those whose minds are too clouded to see what's right in front of them, but I can assure you, child, old Gertie ain't never going to let go of the magic. A world without magic is a very dark world indeed."

"I have to agree." I looked around the charming room. There was something about this space that was so peaceful and serene. "I don't suppose any of your living-impaired friends have mentioned what might have happened to Buck?"

"'Fraid not. But I do know of one man you might want to talk to if you're interested in tracking down Buck's killer. I'm not sayin' he did it, mind you. I'm just sayin' he might have information critical to this particular investigation."

"Who?"

"Toby Upton. Buck and Toby used to be occasional partners, but they had a falling out a while back and went their separate ways."

"So Toby is a treasure hunter like Buck?"

"He tries. Although, unlike Buck, Toby manages to hold down a job at the local grocery in addition to his treasure hunting."

"Do you have any idea what the falling out between them was about?"

"The men partnered up to buy an old map from an antique dealer. Now, it wasn't near as valuable as, say, the map to Barkley's treasure, but had the treasure the map supposedly led to been found, it would have paid for itself a hundred times over."

"They didn't find it?"

"They lost the map. Or, as Toby tells it, Buck lost the map."

"He lost it?"

"In a poker game. Now, I know what you're thinking. Why would a self-proclaimed professional treasure hunter risk a map worth who knows how much on a poker game? The truth of the matter is, Buck didn't always think straight on those unwise occasions when he mixed gambling and alcohol."

"I imagine Toby was upset that Buck had been so careless," I said.

"Upset is too mild a word. Toby was madder than a wet hen and insisted that Buck owed him not only what he'd put out for the map, but half of what the treasure, had they found it, would have been worth. Of course, Buck didn't have any money, so Toby never saw a cent back, but ever since then Toby had been going around town threatening to get even."

"You think it's possible Toby killed Buck over the map?"

Gertie paused. "I don't think he would have come up with a plan to kill Buck that he then carried out, but I can imagine a scenario in which Buck was telling everyone he had the map to Barkley's treasure, causing Toby to follow him to collect what he thought was due him."

"So Toby followed him to Garrett's attic where they got into a tussle, and Buck was killed in the fray?" I finished.

Gertie shrugged. "It's a theory. I'm not even sure it's a good theory, but it might be worth checking out. If Toby didn't kill Buck, he might have some insight as to who might have. Even though the men had a falling out they did tend to travel in the same social circle."

"Do you know where I can find Toby?"

"Like I said, he works at the market."

Our conversation paused as a young couple with two small children came into the diner. Gertie excused herself to take their order at just about the same time Grandpa returned from the bathroom and the group on the deck returned from looking at the boats. I only half-listened to the enthusiastic retelling by the girls of all the awesome crafts they'd seen as I tried to sort out everything that Gertie had shared with me.

When Gertie returned with our food, the conversation naturally segued from a recapping of the boats in the harbor to general chitchat, including a very entertaining description of the social activities available on the island.

"One of the most popular activities during the warmer months is our outdoor theater," Gertie informed us. "Folks gather on the beach and watch a movie that's projected on a large white sail. We don't really have access to new movies, but an old one watched under the stars is a truly magical experience. Folks come from all around to share in the event."

"I wanna go," Gracie chimed in.

"Movies are shown every first and third Wednesday during the summer."

It did my heart good to see Gracie's face light up at the prospect of an outdoor movie. When I was a child growing up in Serenity, the town just at the foot of the mountain had a drive-in movie theater. It had since been torn down, but I still remembered the magic of putting on a pair of PJs, making a paper bag full of homemade popcorn, and heading down the mountain for a double feature. There really was something special about sitting out under the stars as a story unfolded on the big screen in front of you. A movie on the beach sounded like heaven on earth, and I, for one, couldn't wait for Wednesday.

"So I assume this Podunk island doesn't possess an actual movie theater?" Ashley asked rather rudely.

"You would be correct in your assumption," Gertie answered. "However, we do have an awesome community center that holds activities every Friday night for the young folks on the island."

"What kind of activities?" Ashley asked suspiciously.

"This Friday we're having a barbeque for teens and preteens in the sixth to tenth grade."

"I'll be in the sixth grade this year." I noticed a small smile beginning to form in the corners of Ashley's mouth.

"Then you should definitely sign up."

Ashley frowned and forced her face back into a scowl. "Sounds dumb, just like every other dumb thing on this dumb island."

"Ashley," I scolded. "Gertie was just trying to help. I want you to apologize."

Ashley got up from the table, her food untouched. "I hate you, and I hate this island." With that, she stormed out the front door.

"I'm so sorry," I said to Gertie as I began to get up.

Kyle placed his hand on my arm. "I'll get her."

I nodded and turned my attention back to Gertie. "I really do apologize. I know she isn't happy about having her life uprooted for a whole summer, but I don't understand why she's so determined to be miserable. I've tried to talk to her about her attitude toward our adventure, but she's made it clear she isn't buying anything I'm selling. I'm sure she would have a lot of fun at the barbeque, and I do appreciate your mentioning it."

Gertie shrugged. "Kids are angsty by nature even when they aren't angry about something specific, like being dragged to stay with their father's old friend while he's away at a business meeting."

"I wasn't that bad."

"Lordie be, that girl has nothin' on her big sister. I remember you stompin' around town making sure that everyone knew the pain you had suffered. But like you, Ashley's got a big heart and tender soul. Give her time; she'll come around."

"I hope so, for everyone's sake."

Gertie crossed her ample arms across her ample chest. "It'll be easier on her once she makes some friends. There's a wonderful woman who runs a summer kids' camp at the recreation complex on Shell Beach. You might want to look into it."

"That sounds great. Where can I find out more?"

"Just drop by the recreation complex. It's located at the end of the road you drove to reach the resort. Just continue on past the point where you turned off onto the resort road. You can't miss it."

"Thanks. I'll do that. Maybe in a week or two after we've had a chance to settle in."

Gertie shook her head. "I wouldn't be waitin' long. That girl of yours needs to unleash some of the anger that's been building up and the sooner the better."

"Okay, I'll look into it on Monday. I promise."

"Is the camp for kids my age too?" Gracie asked.

"You betcha, sweet cheeks. And it is fun, fun, fun. They even take groups of kids on overnight camping trips. They were going to take a group this week, but it was postponed on account of the special town meeting."

"Town meeting?" I asked.

"I figured you'd know all about it, considering that the topic of conversation is Garrett's land."

"Garrett's land?"

"There's a developer in town who has been going around getting local business owners to sign a petition to try to force Garrett to sell his land to Destination Properties."

I frowned. "Force Garrett to sell? Can they do that?"

Gertie shrugged. "On the surface, it seems Garrett can do what he pleases with the property, but the man who showed up a month or so ago from Destination Properties seemed to have been moderately successful at convincing the business owners to support his bid to buy the land. He's promising everyone huge increases in their bottom lines if they get onboard. The man managed to get enough support that the mayor called the meeting."

"Garrett never said a word about that."

"He might not know. The people who know how to contact him seem bent on protecting him. Still, it does seem the cat would have found its way out of the bag one way or another."

"The man behind this—what's his name?"

"Greg Norton. He's staying over at the inn if you feel the need to have a chat with him."

"I do have a need. A rather large one. Do you have a phone number and address for the inn?"

"I can get if for you. The Gull Island Inn is run by a nice woman named Hallie Bolton. I'll let her know you'll be stopping by."

CHAPTER 3

As soon as we returned from dinner, I called the inn, but Mr. Norton was out, so I decided I'd just stop by the next day. I also wanted to have a conversation with Toby Upton, but I figured speaking to him about a murder with two kids in tow wasn't the best idea, so I decided to table that discussion until the following day as well.

Once I'd gotten the girls settled with their animals in the rooms they had picked out, I headed back downstairs. I was trying to decide if I should start unpacking or just relax when I heard a loud, high-pitched squawking.

"Kill the cat, kill the cat."

I ran downstairs just in time to see my cat, Cuervo, jump from the top of the birdcage, where he must have been harassing the poor bird, and run for cover.

"Are you okay?" I asked Blackbeard.

"Kill the cat, kill the cat."

"How about we move you back to the sunroom? We can get you settled in for the night." I was afraid that moving the extremely large cage back and forth from the living room to the sunroom was going to be a huge pain, but Kyle had found a second cage in Garrett's bedroom that he'd set up in the sunroom. I made sure Blackbeard had plenty of water, as well as a special treat, before I closed the door to the cage, checked and rechecked the latch, covered the cage with the drape Kyle assured me was supposed to be used when the bird slept, then slipped out of the room, closing the door behind me. I was going to have to have a chat with Cuervo about house-guest etiquette and how rude it would be to eat the resident bird, but for now I poured myself a glass of wine and took it out onto the deck.

It was a warm evening with just a tiny breeze. I watched as the waves crashed onto the beach less than a football field away. It had been a hectic and stressful day tacked onto a stressful and hectic few months, but as I watched the sun set into the ocean, I knew I'd found a haven to mend my heart and bring a sense of order back into my life.

Both Grandpa and Doc had retired to their rooms and, as promised, Kyle had gone to fetch enough groceries to see us through a couple of days. Now that we were finally here, the adrenaline I'd existed on ever since I'd made the decision to make the trip east had dissipated, leaving behind a level of fatigue I couldn't quite describe. I'd made the decision to come to the island on a whim after several life-altering events left me feeling unsettled.

My downward spiral began when my longtime boyfriend Hunter Hanson's grandfather, Jake Hanson, passed away two months ago. Jake's health had been failing for quite some time, so his death wasn't unexpected; still, Jake had been one of the town's founding fathers, so his passing had impacted almost everyone I knew in one way or another. The most abrupt change in my own life was to my relationship with Hunter. I loved Hunter, I would always love Hunter, and I knew he loved me, but somehow that was never quite enough for us. I truly believed Hunter and I only continued to move our relationship forward because we both loved Jake, and our eventual nuptials and the prospect of great-grandchildren seemed so important to him. After he passed and the dust settled, Hunter and I had talked and decided to part as friends. On the surface this shouldn't have caused the emotional roller coaster I'd experienced since the breakup, but when Hunter began dating the new pediatrician in town shortly after we split, emotions I hadn't even known I'd been holding at bay gushed forth in one big burst of instability.

Of course, the real reason I headed for the east coast at the drop of a hat, had more to do with my father's recent engagement. Don't get me wrong, I loved my dad and I was happy that he had found love after so many years of being single. The problem wasn't that my dad was planning a life with the woman he'd been dating for the past few years; it was that the girls and I lived at the resort with my dad, and the new living arrangement left me feeling like a third wheel. When I'd heard about Garrett's need for someone to oversee the resort renovations, I'd jumped at the opportunity to take a step away from what had become my very complicated and confusing life.

Of course, now that I was here and I'd seen firsthand how my spontaneous decision had affected my sisters, I had to wonder if I hadn't just made the biggest mistake of my life.

Echo put his head in my lap as if sensing my discontent. He was a sensitive dog who seemed well equipped to read my many moods. Bernese Mountain Dogs tended to be in tune with their human's needs anyway, but Echo and I were a search-and-rescue team, which created a heightened level of bonding.

"What do you think?" I asked my furry friend. "Was I rash in bringing us here for the summer?"

Echo lifted his head from my lap. He picked my cell up off the table and brought it to me.

"You think I should call Jenna?"

Echo put his paw on my lap.

"It's kind of late."

Echo barked once.

"Of course, with the time difference, it isn't so late at Paradise Lake."

I pulled up my best friend Jenna Elston's number and hit enter. Jenna and I had been best friends since preschool when I tried to steal her red crayon. Instead of lashing out, Jenna had befriended me and we'd been best friends ever since.

"Oh my God. I'm so glad you called," Jenna answered after the first ring. "I was just thinking about you. You must have read my mind."

"Actually Echo read your mind, but I'm really happy I decided to call too."

"So how is South Carolina? Is it romantic? I bet it's romantic."

I could almost see Jenna's blue eyes flash with enthusiasm as I looked out at the sea. It was a warm summer night that seemed to wrap me in a hug as I listened to the crickets in the background.

"Actually," I answered, "it is romantic. Not that I have anyone to be romantic with."

"Are you sure?" Jenna asked.

I knew she meant Kyle. Jenna had been hinting for months that perhaps the love of my life hadn't been Hunter, but the man who had been standing beside me all along.

"We've talked about this before. Kyle and I are just friends, and the fact that Hunter and I have officially split doesn't change that in the least."

"Not that I believe you, because deep down you must realize that you are supposed to end up with Kyle, but we've been over this before and I really want to hear about your trip. Tell me everything. What is the most amazing thing that has happened to you so far?"

"Kyle and I found a body in the attic."

I waited during the long pause. "A real one?" she asked.

"Afraid so."

I spent the next twenty minutes sharing everything I knew about Buck and his search for a mythical treasure with Jenna, who interrupted the flow of the retelling on several occasions with questions of her own.

"Are you are going to investigate?"

"Actually, probably not. I have a resort to refurbish and sisters to look after. I doubt I'll have time for much else."

Jenna just laughed.

"What's so funny?" I asked.

"You telling me that you don't plan to investigate. It's hysterical."

"Why? I don't even know the guy."

"Maybe, but I bet that mind of yours has already been listing suspects, categorizing details, and formatting questions. I have known you almost your entire life, and if there is one thing I know to be true, it's that if there is a puzzle to solve Tj Jensen is going to be the one to solve it."

"Not always."

"Always."

Jenna did have a point. I think one of the reasons I found myself involved in so many mysteries was because of my innate need to figure things out. "So how are things in Serenity?" I decided to change the subject rather than admit that Jenna knew me as well as she thought she knew me.

"Okay."

I could tell by Jenna's tone of voice that her "okay" really meant the opposite. "What's wrong?"

"Nothing really."

"Come on, Jen. A best friend knows when something's wrong."

"It's not any one thing. It's a bunch of little things that have teamed up to bring stress and aggravation into my life."

"Such as?"

I listened while Jenna let out a long breath. "Probably the biggest thing at the moment is time. The restaurant has been super busy so I've been working a lot of hours, which can be expected since summers are always busy. I guess the bigger issue has to do with Dennis's promotion." Jenna's husband was a firefighter. "Now that he's made Captain, he's been working a lot of hours too. Between the two of us we've been working too many hours. I barely ever see Dennis and the girls are spending most of the summer with a babysitter. I love my family and I love my life, but I have to admit that I'm a little jealous of your adventure."

"I wouldn't be too jealous if I were you. So far my adventure has consisted of emotionally distraught sisters, a body in the attic, and a developer who I sense is going to make my life difficult. Not exactly the thing dreams are made of."

"Maybe not, but you took a chance and shook things up. I feel like I'm in a rut."

"Yeah, I get it. Although at the moment, I envy your rut. When I made the decision to come to Gull Island I really thought it was the right thing to do, but now I'm not so sure. I'm really afraid I might have made a mistake."

"It was the right thing," Jenna assured me. "You needed time away to gain perspective after your breakup with Hunter."

"Which is another thing I've been questioning."

"Sweetie, I love you and I love Hunter, but I don't think you did the wrong thing. I know that when you first got back together with Hunter I was your biggest cheerleader. You and Hunter and Dennis and I have a long history filled with fond memories that I will always cherish. All through high school we were like the four Musketeers. Our team meant a lot to me, and

I will admit that the four of us being the four of us again really appealed to me when you first started dating again. But now that I've had a chance to step back and really look at things, I can see that, although you both really tried, there just wasn't a spark."

"We had a spark."

"Not the way you should have. Not the way you do with Kyle."

I sighed. "I told you, Kyle and I are just friends."

"Deny it as long as you want, but a best friend knows these things. I've seen the way he looks at you, and I've seen the way you look at him. I know how important Hunter is to you, but even if there isn't anything between you and Kyle I don't think you and Hunter would have lasted the test of time. If Jake hadn't been in the picture you probably wouldn't have lasted as long as you did."

Jenna was right. Hunter and I might have had a spark in the past, but somewhere along the line that spark had faded. If it hadn't been for Jake, we most likely would have seen that. Somehow my love for Jake and my feelings for Hunter were all wrapped up together.

"Your dad and Rosalie came into the restaurant today." Jenna had obviously decided to change the subject, which was more than fine with me.

"How'd they seem?"

"Happy."

"I know my desertion on the tail of Dad's announcement makes it seem as if I'm upset about the fact that they're finally getting married, but I'm not. It's more that I'm feeling displaced."

"I've known your dad my whole life and I've known Rosalie for years, and based on what I know of both of them, I honestly would be surprised if it even entered either of their minds that you and the girls would move out. You're a family. A big and loving multi-generation family who has made it work for a lot of years."

"I know you're right. My feeling like a third wheel isn't due to anything that either Dad or Rosalie said. I guess I just need some time to get used to all the changes."

"Which, as I said before, was a good move. Relax and try to enjoy your time on the island."

Jenna and I chatted a few more minutes before I heard a crash in the background and Jenna informed me that she had to go clean up the mess their new puppy had made in the kitchen.

I was trying to decide whether to head upstairs or go for a walk when I heard someone ring the doorbell. I got up and went through the house to the front, where I opened the door to Deputy Savage.

"Deputy. What can I do for you?"

"I need to take another look at the attic. It seems we may have new information regarding Buck Barnes's death."

"Really? That was fast. Care to share?"

"No, ma'am. I'll just be a minute."

I stepped aside and let him in. "I spoke to Garrett after you left earlier. He seems to think Buck was killed while looking for the map his father used to own."

"That's a theory."

"Do you have a better one?"

Deputy Savage smiled. "I appreciate your interest, but I'm afraid I can't discuss an open investigation with you. Now, if you'll excuse me, I'll show myself upstairs."

Jenna was right. I did like to be the one to solve a puzzle and being on the outside when I was used to being on the inside was not sitting well with me. I decided to power up my computer and see what I could find out about Buck Barnes. I wasn't the wiz Kyle was at digging up information, but I was resourceful and therefore certain I could dig up the basics in the very least.

As it turned out, Buck was a sixty-eight-year-old lifetime resident of Gull Island who never married and never had children. As far as I could tell, his parents were both deceased and he had no siblings. His work history was pretty much nonexistent, so I had to wonder how he had supported himself. Although, I did remember Gertie commenting that the residents of the island gave the man work sweeping up and such. I suppose he must have been paid under the table since I couldn't find any employment records. There wasn't a lot of information about the man on the web, but he was briefly mentioned in an article for a popular magazine who had done a feature on Gull Island and the treasure hunters who seemed to gravitate to the island.

The longer I searched, the more convinced I was that the answers I was looking for would not be found on the information highway known as the World Wide Web. It looked as if the answers I sought would be found the old fashion way, direct conversations with the people who knew the man and called him friend. It was late and I was ready to turn in, but tomorrow I'd put on my sleuthing hat and see what I could dig up.

CHAPTER 4

Monday, June 19

In spite of my best intentions, I hadn't followed up with any of the people I planned to follow up with after the events of Friday. Kyle suggested we should get everything unpacked and put away so that we'd feel more settled. His idea made sense, so we made it a priority on Saturday morning to relax and get to know our home for the summer. Of course, when we found that the guest shower leaked and the garbage disposal sent food hurling into the kitchen rather than taking waste the opposite direction, our priorities changed considerably. Saturday became devoted to making the house livable, so any unpacking that needed to be done was pushed off to Sunday.

Monday began for me as the sky was just beginning to turn light. I woke early and quietly gathered the household's three dogs and headed downstairs. I figured a leisurely walk on the beach would go a long way toward quieting my mind. I let the warm water wash over my feet as the dogs chased the seagulls who were scavenging for their morning meal during low tide. I felt myself begin to relax as I focused on the sound of the waves crashing onto the shore as the sun began to rise. It was nice to have the beach to myself as I looked toward the day ahead.

Although I had been busy all weekend, I'd still spent a considerable amount of time thinking about Buck's murder. The method by which Deputy Savage seemed to be investigating was unusual at best. He'd never even sent a crime scene team over. Even Deputy Roy Fisher back home, who admittedly wasn't the brightest cop in the world, knew to send people around to check for fingerprints and other physical evidence. I was sure that Deputy Savage wasn't as inept as he seemed. Different law enforcement agencies had different procedures, and I knew I just needed to accept that. Besides, I knew that Savage wouldn't want me getting involved in his investigation, and I wasn't sure I wanted to get involved, but I was certain there wasn't any harm in taking some time to introduce myself to some of the residents of the island. Gertie had mentioned Buck's ex-partner Toby Upton as a suspect in Buck's death. It made sense, I suppose, that if Toby felt Buck owed him a debt he might feel he was due a piece of any new treasure Buck might stumble onto. I didn't know for certain that Toby had followed Buck to the attic, struggled with him, and ended up killing him, as Gertie suggested, but I was sure no harm could come from introducing myself to the man and letting the conversation take us where it would.

As the dogs and I wandered toward the south end of the beach, I noticed roped-off areas that indicated there were turtles nesting. I was anxious to speak to Meg from the turtle rescue squad about what we could do to help ensure that as many of the hatchlings as possible made it safely into the sea. I'd done a bit of reading about the struggle to protect the endangered turtles and only a very small percentage of eggs actually ended up as adult turtles. I could understand why Garrett was so intent on making sure the land his family had owned and protected for generations continued to remain intact and unhindered by development after he was gone. It seemed to me that as Garrett's representative while he was away it was imperative of me to track down this Norton fellow and have a chat about his plans.

It was still early when the dogs and I returned to the house, so I fed the animals, showered, and dressed in a pair of shorts and a tank top. In all I had three people on my list to speak to: Toby Upton, Greg Norton, and Meg from the museum. I doubted that the museum would be open yet, so after leaving a note for the other members of the household, all of whom were still sleeping, I headed into town in the hope of speaking to both Toby Upton and Greg Norton.

The small touristy town was charming. Most of the businesses displayed colorful flowers in barrels in front of their storefronts, and many had awnings with blue and white stripes over the entries as well. The harbor was just across the street from the main thoroughfare, providing the atmospheric sound of seagulls and picturesque beauty of fishing boats in the background.

I decided to stop by the Gull Island Inn first in hopes of catching Mr. Norton before he headed out for the day. The inn itself was lovely. A lush green lawn bordered by a colorful flower garden and wraparound porch greeted me as I walked up the cobblestone walkway to the double front door. I imagined many guests had whiled away a summer evening sitting in one of the rocking chairs that were arranged artfully along the front of the building.

One of the fondest memories I had of my grandmother was the image of her sitting on the front porch of the house at the resort watching the sunset from the rocker my grandfather had made for one of her birthdays. I'd head outside and sit on one of the hardwood benches that lined the railing while Grandma would tell me stories of growing up in a wealthy family from the big city. She'd given up so much to move to the one-room cabin my grandfather had owned when they'd first met. I'd often wondered if she ever regretted her decision to give up a life of privilege to move to Paradise Lake, but looking back on the time we spent together, you only had to notice the love radiating from her eyes to know that she was happy and content with the life she'd chosen.

I climbed the three steps to the front door and knocked.

"Can I help you?" a friendly-looking woman with a huge smile and a sparkle in her eye inquired.

"My name is Tj Jensen."

"The woman staying out at Garrett's place. I heard you'd arrived." The woman's bracelets, which matched her long peasant dress, jangled as she reached out to shake my hand. I had to admit the local gossip hotline really was impressive. Everyone I'd spoken to so far seemed to know exactly who I was. "My name is Hallie Bolton. Please do come in. Gertie called to tell me you'd be by. She said I should tell you everything I know and help in any way I can."

"That was nice of her."

"Gertie can be caustic if you get on her bad side, but if she likes you she'll move heaven and earth to help you, and it was clear to me she really likes you. Besides, I want to help, although I'm afraid you've missed Mr. Norton."

"I'm sorry to hear that. I hoped to discuss his plans for Garrett's property with him."

"You might want to check out the coffee bar down the street. He's been known to stop by for a beverage in the morning."

"I could use some coffee. Can you point me in the right direction?"

"Just take a left when you go out the door. Marina Coffee is about two blocks down on your right. You can't miss it; there's a giant cup of coffee painted on the front window."

"Thanks." I hesitated. "Was Gertie right that Mr. Norton has been successful in his bid to convince the town to rally together to pressure Garrett into selling the Turtle Cove Resort to Destination Properties?"

"The man *is* persuasive, and there are those who have come around to his way of thinking. There's no doubt that the sale would change the culture of the island considerably."

"And there are those who support that change?"

Hallie nodded. "I'm afraid the locals are very much divided in their opinions as to whether a megaresort would benefit or destroy the island. There are those, like Gertie and me, who live on Gull Island because we enjoy the small-town feel. For us, island life is ideal with its slower pace and easygoing way of life. There are others, however, who find it difficult to make a living with the tourist base we currently enjoy. Norton is promising a megaresort with a room capacity of over two hundred. He's managed to convince many of the small business owners there'll be a huge payday when it's completed and the rooms are filled."

"I guess I can see how an increase in revenue might be appealing to some, but Garrett is pretty adamant about not wanting to sell to a large corporation."

"Personally, I hope he fights for the resort, but I'm afraid that if enough of his friends and neighbors agree that a megaresort will be good for the island I can see Garrett giving in. He cares about the resort and the environment, but he cares about his friends as well. You really should come to the town meeting on Thursday so you have a better idea of what the whole thing is about."

"I intend to. Thank you for your time."

After leaving the inn I headed toward the coffee bar. The downtown section of Gull Island was beginning to come to life as the small mom-and-pop shops along the main drag began to open their doors for the day. I greeted several shop owners who were sweeping up in front of their doors or watering the flowers that grew along the walkway. I really enjoyed the town's beachy feel, with seagulls flying overhead and local vendors displaying racks of surfboards, bathing suits, and other items one would need for a day by the sea.

There was a long line when I arrived at Marina Coffee, so I headed to the back of it and took in the friendly nature of the customers while I waited. The crowd who met in the coffee bar seemed to be a festive group who chatted about the weather and local events. It almost felt like a gathering you'd see in someone's kitchen, and I noticed the woman taking the orders seemed to greet most of the customers by name.

"What'll ya have, sugar?" she asked when it was my turn.

"Nonfat no foam latte."

"Name?"

"Tj."

The woman wrote my name on the cup.

"Muffin?"

"Apricot."

The woman handed me the freshly made treat. "Anything else?"

"No, although I was hoping you could help me with something. I was just talking to Hallie down at the inn and she mentioned I might be able to find Greg Norton here."

"Sorry, sugar; he's been and gone." The woman poured steamed milk into my cup.

"Do you happen to know where I might find him now?"

"He didn't say. That'll be seven-fifty."

I paid the woman and then looked at my watch. I really wanted to take Ashley and Gracie to the kids' camp this morning, so tracking down everyone I wanted to speak to would have to wait, but maybe I could fit one more visit into my morning schedule.

The Gull Island Market was small, with an abundance of delicious-looking fresh produce artfully displayed at the front of the brick building. I'd been craving some fresh fruit so I made a mental note to come back when I had more time to shop. Right now I had an interview to conduct with the first and only suspect on my list.

"Excuse me," I addressed the sleepy-looking woman at the checkout counter. "I'm looking for Toby Upton."

"In the back, unpacking boxes."

I looked toward the rear of the store, where a hallway, which I assumed led to the back, was clearly marked as providing restrooms. "Is it okay to go on back?"

"Fine by me."

I smiled at the woman, who looked bored, bored, bored, before heading to the rear of the store, which appeared to be free of customers. Luckily, there was only one person in the back, an older man with a slight hump in his back. "Are you Toby Upton?"

"Who's askin'?"

"Tj Jensen. I was hoping to speak to you about Buck Barnes."

"Don't have nothin' to say about that no-good backstabbin' thief."

"I guess you heard he's dead."

"Yeah. So?"

"There are those who think you might have had a hand in it."

Toby laughed. "Trust me, I had no use for a man who tried to swindle me out of what he owed me, but I didn't kill him.

Why would I? Now that the blackheart is dead there's no way for me to ever collect what I'm due."

I supposed Toby had a point. "Do you know who might have wanted him dead?"

"Lots of folks."

"Such as?"

Toby set down the box cutter he'd been holding and hoisted himself up onto a counter. I guess he figured if we were going to chat he'd make himself comfortable. "Tara Lee Bradford, for one."

"Who is she and why would she want Buck dead?"

"Tara Lee owns one of those big homes up on the bluff with the fancy landscaping. Buck got it in his head that there was treasure buried on her property, so he took to sneaking over her wall at night and digging in her flower bed. Wowie, talk about mad. I thought Tara Lee was going to skin the man alive right there in the middle of the town square after she realized he was the one responsible for digging up several of her prize roses."

"Do you think this Tara Lee would follow Buck to Garrett Hanford's house and kill him in the attic?"

Toby scrunched up his nose. "No, I don't suppose she would."

"Did Buck tell you he'd found Garrett's map?"

"He told everyone he'd found the map. 'Course, everyone knew the map was long gone. Garrett told me so himself a long time ago."

"Can you think of anyone who might have believed Buck and followed him to the attic?"

Toby jumped down off the counter and picked up his box cutter. "I best get back to work, but I guess it wouldn't hurt to have a conversation with a man named Adam Joyner. I heard he teamed up with Buck shortly before Buck disappeared."

"Do you know where I can find Mr. Joyner?"

"He works at the post office."

"Is there anyone else you can think of that I might want to speak to?"

"Nope."

I left the store and returned to my car. I did need to get home, but I supposed it wouldn't hurt to stop by and see if Gertie had any news. Before we'd left on Friday she'd promised to keep her ear to the ground, and I'd come to learn that if there was news on the island to be had, Gertie was the one who was apt to have it.

"I was just thinking about you and here you are," Gertie greeted me when I walked in. She turned to the woman who was sitting at the counter. "This here is the sweet little thing I was telling you about."

"I'm so happy to meet you." The woman smiled. "My name is Beverly, although most people call me Bev."

"I'm Tj."

"Gertie here was telling me that you are planning to take on Greg Norton and the development he works for," Bev informed me.

"It is my intention to speak to the man if I can ever track him down and make certain that Garrett's wishes are made clear. I went by the inn this morning, but he had already left."

Beverly motioned for me to have a seat on the stool beside her.

"That man is bad news. If you ask me, he'll do anything he needs to do to get Garrett's land. I guess you heard that he's been seen loitering around at the resort?"

"Loitering around? What do you mean? What has he been doing?"

"I'm not sure exactly, but I'm willin' to bet he's been up to no good. I've done some checking and it seems that Destination Properties, the company he works for, has a reputation for buying land at a discount after some sort of problem with the property has been discovered."

"You're suggesting Norton creates the problems in the first place?"

"That would be my guess. Of course, I have nothing to base that on other than a hunch, but if it were me trying to protect Garrett's property, I'd keep my eyes open."

"Okay, thanks, I will. Do you happen to know who it was that had seen him at the resort?"

"Meg from over at the museum is the one that mentioned it to me, so I'd speak to her."

"I will."

"Any news about Buck's murder?" Gertie asked.

"Not really. I stopped by and spoke to Toby. Like you said, he was pretty mad at Buck, but I doubt he's our killer. For one thing, I don't think he's physically capable of hitting a man hard enough to kill him. He did give me another name, however. Adam Joyner."

Gertie frowned. "I know that Buck convinced Adam to take a leave of absence from his job to help him look for treasure, but I don't see Adam as the sort to kill a person."

"I don't know," Beverly countered. "The popular theory is that Adam suffered some sort of a breakdown."

"Breakdown?" I asked.

"Adam is a married man with a good job and three children to support," Gertie explained. "I'm not sure how Buck did it, but somehow he managed to convince Adam to temporarily chuck it all to go treasure hunting. I suppose Adam must have been going through a bit of a midlife crisis and needed a break from the monotony and responsibility of his life, and a treasure hunt was a way to take that break. Chances are that Adam would have worked through the temporary insanity that caused him to do such a thing in fairly short order on his own, but Adam's wife,

Beth, was having none of it. The last time I saw her, she was on her way to knock Buck upside the head and put a stop to the whole thing."

"And did she?"

"I guess she must have. Adam is back at work at the post office."

"Did Buck do that often?" I asked Bev. "Talk people into joining his treasure hunt?"

"Buck was a friendly sort who had a tendency to make friends fairly easy, and it was natural for him to want to share his passion for treasure hunting with a lot of different people. I can think of a handful of people who caught the fever from Buck, but Buck never really had the financial resources to make his dream into a reality and most of the local folks on the island knew that."

"Garrett seems to think that Buck was killed as a result of partnering up with the wrong person."

"I sort of doubt that," Bev answered. "Although there are folks in town who are speculating that Buck might actually have found the map he was going around telling everyone he had. I suppose if that were true he could have partnered up with the wrong person. Unfortunately, he didn't have the mechanism in his brain that allows most of us to discriminate between individuals who would make good friends and those it would be best to avoid."

"You said that Beth Joyner planned to knock Buck upside the head. You don't think she actually did so?"

"Beth?" Bev shook her head. "Beth is a strong woman who likes to keep a tight rein on the finances since Adam tends to go off on a tangent every now and then, but I don't see her killing a man over something like a treasure hunt. No, if you ask me, it's more likely that Buck was killed by someone from out of the area."

"I had seen him hanging out with a couple of men," Gertie added.

"Do you know their names?"

"No," Gertie answered. "I can't say I ever caught a name. I can ask around and see what I can dig up if you'd like."

"Thanks. That would be helpful just in case we decide we need the information at some point in the future." I glanced at the clock. "It was nice chatting with you both, but I have to go. I'm taking the girls to kids' camp today."

The girls were still getting ready for kids' camp when I returned home, so I took out the small notebook and turned to a clean page. I settled onto a bar stool and wrote: "Who killed Buck Barnes?"

I then created two columns: "Suspect" and "Motive."

In the first column, I jotted down, "Toby Upton." Next to his name I wrote: "Buck owed him money." Under Toby's name I wrote "Beth Joyner." Next to her name I added: "Husband talked into joining Buck's treasure hunt." I figured Beth had a pretty good motive for wanting Buck out of the way. Trying to pay the bills and raise three children while your husband was off on a treasure hunt couldn't be easy, and Gertie did say that the last time she spoke to Beth she was on her way to hit Buck upside the head. Neither Gertie nor Bev seemed to think that she'd actually killed Buck, but in my mind it wasn't outside the realm of possibility that she had actually carried through with her threat.

Under Beth's name I wrote "Adam Joyner." I wasn't sure if he had a motive, but if he was mixed up with Buck just prior to his death, that made him a suspect.

At the bottom of the list I added Greg Norton's name. Under motive I wrote "wants Garrett's land." It occurred to me that if Norton had been out at the resort doing whatever it was that he planned to do to decrease the value of Garrett's property, perhaps Buck had been out at the resort looking for the map at the same time and had seen something that Norton didn't want seen. I'd never even met the man, but based on what I'd heard about him, I was willing to bet that Norton might be willing to kill a man if it meant getting what he wanted.

If I was totally honest, I really hoped that Norton was our guy. I currently felt my attention was split in many different directions, but if the man who was trying to steal Garrett's land was also our killer, it would lessen the burden significantly.

Once the list was made I highlighted Toby's name with a yellow marker. I decided that I'd color code my suspects as I worked. If the suspect seemed innocent, but I didn't know for certain, I'd highlight them in yellow. If I'd all but cleared them, I'd highlight them in green, and if after speaking to them they remained firmly at the top of my list, I'd highlight them in red.

I didn't have an alibi for Toby, but because I didn't know exactly when Buck had been killed, trying to confirm alibis wasn't going to work in this case. Toby didn't look like he could physically overtake and kill a man, and he hadn't seemed the least bit secretive in his replies, so I pretty much doubted he was the one I was looking for.

I added Tara Lee's name on a separate page. I doubted she was the one who'd killed Buck, but Toby had mentioned her as a suspect and you never knew when you might have cause to follow up on a statement someone you'd spoken to had made. I also added Meg from the museum to this second list. I had no reason to believe she was responsible for Buck's death, but if she knew the identity of the person or persons who had seen Norton on the property she might be able to provide a valuable clue.

I wished I had more time to develop my list, but my sisters appeared from upstairs once I'd entered Meg's name into my notebook, and helping them find a comfortable routine for the summer was the most important thing at the moment.

CHAPTER 5

It had taken quite a bit of negotiating to get Ashley and Gracie to agree to check out the Gull Island Kids' Camp. Ashley was still pretty committed to her agenda of making my life miserable by hating every single thing about the island, and Gracie was so insecure that she almost broke into tears at the thought of being left alone in a strange environment. After I assured them both that not only was Uncle Kyle coming with us, but that I also wouldn't force them to stay at the camp if they weren't so inclined, they both agreed to give it a try.

"Wow, this looks really nice," I commented as we pulled up in front of a large wooden building right on the beach. The facility was situated so that a wall of windows looked out onto a pool that divided the grassy area where soccer and baseball fields were set up, the ocean just beyond. There were rows of volleyball nets lined up along the beach and colorful rowboats tied to buoys just offshore.

"It's okay," Ashley agreed. "Did we bring swimsuits?"

"You each have your backpack with a swimsuit, a towel, sunscreen, a snack, and a water bottle, just in case you decide to stay."

It was obvious by the look of terror on Gracie's face that

even the prospect of swimming in the Olympic-sized pool wasn't going to be enough to convince her to spend the day at the camp. I had to admit that despite the fact that Ashley had become a huge pain in my backside with her frequent outbursts, I was much more concerned about my younger sister, Gracie. When Ashley and Gracie had first come to live with me after our mother died, Ashley had refused to accept the fact that Mom was never coming back and spent months making sure everyone in her orbit was as miserable as she was. In comparison, Gracie seemed to make the best of her new situation after only a brief period of adjustment. I had hoped her willingness to adapt to new situations would carry through on our trip to the island, but so far she seemed to be having an even harder time than Ashley.

"Let's go inside to talk to the director so we can see what this is all about," Kyle suggested.

"Okay, but remember, we don't have to stay," Gracie reminded him.

"Got it. This is just a recon mission."

"What's recon?"

"It's an investigation to see what's what. Sort of like spying."

That had Gracie giggling.

Gracie loved Kyle. Don't get me wrong: we all loved Kyle. He had to be one of the kindest people on the planet, but Gracie seemed to have forged a special bond with the man who, I suspected, had become some sort of surrogate father to her in her young mind. Not that I minded. If Gracie was going to attach herself to any man, Kyle was a wonderful choice. But I did worry about what would happen if, for whatever reason, he was no longer in our lives.

"I hope this isn't some lame camp for little kids," Ashley commented as we walked across the parking lot toward the large structure.

"Gertie made it sound like the camp catered to kids of all ages."

"I don't need a babysitter."

"I know that. It never occurred to me that you did. But it might be fun to have something to do every day other than hang out at the resort *literally* watching the paint dry."

"Lame." Ashley rolled her eyes at my attempt at a joke.

A rush of cool air greeted us as we opened the front door. I was still getting used to the fact that most of the buildings on the island had been outfitted with air conditioners that I imagined ran continuously throughout the summer. Having grown up in the mountains, with a much cooler climate, the centrally cooled air was something I would have to get used to.

In the lobby we were greeted by a woman who looked to be around my age. She had dark hair that she wore in a long braid over one shoulder. Like me, she had a smattering of freckles across her nose and, also like me, she was petite and totally devoid of makeup.

"Welcome. My name is Willow. I'm the director of the Gull Island Kids' Camp. How can I help you?"

"This is Ashley and Gracie. We're going to be spending the summer on the island, and Gertie, from the diner, suggested we check out your program."

"You must be the wonderful friend who has given up her summer to help Garret with his renovations."

I nodded. Did everyone know Garrett had asked me to help out? "My name is Tj, and this is Kyle."

"So very happy to meet you, Kyle."

Willow's eyes seemed to dance with delight when she spoke. Of course, Kyle tended to receive enthusiastic greetings from all the women he was introduced to. Although if you asked me, he never seemed to notice the stir he created with his exceptional good looks.

"Do you know Garrett well?" I wondered.

"We're friends. We share a common love of old black and white movies, turtle rescue, and sappy novels."

Sappy novels? This was something I didn't know about my father's longtime friend. "You have a beautiful facility. It's very inviting, and I love the view of the ocean just outside the windows."

"Thank you. We consider ourselves to be very fortunate. Our land was donated for use as a recreational facility by one of our oldest families, and the entire island pitched in to raise the funds we needed for the building." Willow came out from behind the counter and turned her attention to the girls. "So, how old are the two of you?"

"Eleven," Ashley answered.

"Eight," Gracie answered in turn.

"That's perfect. We cater to both island residents and visitors between the ages of six and sixteen. Our campers are grouped by age: six through nine, ten through twelve, and thirteen through sixteen. The older group is more often than not engaged in activities off-site such as sailing or scuba diving, while the two younger groups spend the majority of the time at the facility. We do, however, have a wonderful surfing program that anyone who can pass the swim test can sign up for, and we also have craft rooms, an exercise room, and a computer lab inside, although our computer lab is down at the moment. Seems our system crashed and I haven't had a chance to have it looked at yet."

"You have a centralized server with work stations?" Kyle verified.

"We do."

"I can take a look at it, if you'd like."

"Kyle is a whiz with computers," I assured the friendly woman.

"Really? That would be great. I've been trying to get someone out to look at it since last Friday."

Kyle turned to look at me. "Why don't you go ahead and take Ben into town as planned? I'll look at the server and then just hang out here with the girls for a few hours. You can pick us up later in the day, if that's okay with Willow."

"That's more than okay." Willow grinned. "If Ashley and Gracie decide to continue with the program we'll need to have you fill out information packets," she informed me. "They're mainly to ensure we have medical information and emergency contacts. I'll send them home with the girls and you can look them over this evening."

"I'll do that. By the way, can you tell me where I can find a pharmacy in town?"

"There's only one. It's in the same building as the barbershop on Cove Street, which is where you'll find most of the services you'd need as a resident, such as the dry cleaners, the medical building, and the hair salon. It's the next street up from Bayview."

"Do you have all the information you'll need?" I asked Grandpa as we headed out the front door of the house at the resort toward my car.

"I do. I called and spoke to my doctor as well. He's going to send my prescription to the pharmacy once we get a phone number to send it to."

"That's good. It should speed things up a bit."

"How'd the girls like the camp?"

"They were a little unsure about it at first, but they agreed to stay when they found out Kyle would be staying as well."

"That's good. I think Gracie is having a hard time with the changes. I heard her on the phone with your dad this morning."

"She called Dad? When?"

"It was around eight o'clock."

I grimaced. If it was eight o'clock here it would have been five a.m. at home. I'd need to go over the time change again with the girls so my dad's sleep wasn't disturbed on a regular basis. "Did you happen to overhear what they were talking about?"

"Gracie wanted to be sure your dad remembered to water your mom's tree."

I felt my heart break. Poor Gracie. Shortly after my mom was killed in a car accident along with her third husband, Ashley and Gracie had come to live with me. After we'd settled in at Maggie's Hideaway, my dad's resort, we'd planted a tree in memory of our mother. Ashley had cried a few tears at the time, but hadn't seemed overly moved by the tribute. Gracie had visited the tree every day for months afterward. In fact, visiting the tree was one of the last things she'd done prior to our leaving on this trip.

"I think you need to turn left on this next street," Grandpa instructed.

"Yeah, I see it."

The Gull Island Pharmacy and Barber Shop was quaint and old-fashioned and one of the few places other than Gertie's place that I actually remembered from my previous trip to the island. I'd been having one of my tantrums and had locked myself in the attic, but the temperature had really climbed and Garrett wasn't comfortable letting me hide out where there was no air conditioning. Somehow he'd talked me into coming out for a double-decker ice cream cone. I remembered how welcoming the place felt. Not only was there a red-and-white barber pole out in front, but when you walked inside you were greeted by a shop from the past, with two barber chairs to the right and an old-fashioned ice cream counter to the left. If you continued on into the cozy shop you found several aisles of merchandise before arriving at the pharmacy counter in the very back of the store.

"Mr. Brolin," I greeted.

"Can I help you?" a pleasantly plump man with white hair and a neatly trimmed white beard inquired.

"I'm Tj Jensen. My dad is a friend of Garrett's. We met a very long time ago when I came to stay with Garrett while my dad was at a conference."

"I remember you. You wanted to stay in the attic until it was time for you to go home."

"Yeah." I laughed. "Not my finest moment. I do remember that your ice cream got me out of the attic on several occasions though."

"Folks do tend to like my ice cream. I make it fresh, you know."

"I remember."

"So what can I do for you today?"

I stepped aside so that Grandpa could step up to the counter to speak to the man whose eyes, while faded with age, were still bright and welcoming.

"I'm new to Gull Island. I plan to be here for several months, so I'd like to see about having my prescriptions transferred from my regular pharmacy in Nevada." Grandpa took a piece of paper from his pocket on which he'd written down all his medications and handed it to the man behind the counter. "My current address and telephone number as well as the telephone number of my doctor back home are listed on the bottom."

The pharmacist looked at the paper Grandpa handed him and then handed Grandpa a one-page form and a pen. "I'll need you to fill out some paperwork, but we should be able to make the transfer without any problem."

"I'm going to have to bring my sisters in for a cone," I

commented as I waited for Grandpa to fill out the form. "I forgot how much I loved this place until I walked in the door and all sorts of happy memories came flooding back. You know, if you had asked me a week ago I'd have told you I didn't have any happy memories of that summer, but I guess I was wrong."

"That's the way with memories. They aren't always reliable."

"Until you revisit them," I added.

"Gull Island is a special place. There can be challenges inherent in living on an island, but I wouldn't change a thing."

"I understand that there's a man in town trying to get everyone to pressure Garrett into selling his land to a development company. What do you think?"

The pharmacist frowned. "The man has been a thorn in my side since he's been here. Things are fine the way they are. Don't know why everyone is so intent on changing things."

"I was hoping to speak to Mr. Norton before the town meeting on Thursday. I don't suppose you know where I can find him?"

George shook his head. "Sorry. Once I convinced the man I wasn't on board with his proposal and never would be, he quit coming around. If I had to guess, I'd say he's busy working on the undecideds."

I supposed that made sense. There would be those who supported the project and those, like George Brolin and Hallie, who were firmly against. It was those in the middle who had the most potential to affect the overall strength of the petition. "Do you know who these undecided businesses are?"

"The doughnut shop down the street, the sandwich shop next door, and the t-shirt shop on Cove are a start. If you want to have a chance to have your side heard, you'd best come to the town meeting on Thursday."

"I can assure you I intend to."

Grandpa handed George the filled-out form. The pharmacist looked it over and assured us the transfer could be completed by the end of the day. "I suppose if you really want to track Norton down you can try Sully's," George informed us. "It's a local bar a few blocks over. Norton has been known to pop in for a cold one at this time of day."

"Thanks. I'll check it out."

Grandpa and I said our goodbyes after another customer walked in, and George promised to call when the prescriptions were ready to be picked up.

"Do you think Garrett knows anything about this petition?" Grandpa asked.

I'd been asking myself that same question ever since Gertie had told me what Greg Norton was up to. "I don't know for certain, but he hasn't mentioned it so I'm thinking no. I'm trying to decide if I should fill him in. On one hand I feel like he has the right to know, but on the other I don't want to add any more stress to his life."

Grandpa opened the passenger door to the car and slid inside. "Maybe you should go to the meeting on Thursday and then decide."

"Yeah, that's what I've been thinking. I met a woman this morning at Gertie's who said that Norton has been seen loitering around the resort. She told me that Norton is known for buying distressed properties, and it was her impression that he and his company might be responsible for the properties being distressed in the first place."

"Seem like something you might want to have our resident computer genius to look in to."

"That's a good idea. I'll talk to Kyle about it. He really is good at digging around on the web. I'm sure if there is something to find he'll find it." I started the car and adjusted my mirrors before pulling into traffic. "Mr. Brolin said we might find Norton at Sully's. Do you mind if we stop by? I'll buy you a beer."

"Make it a soda and you have a deal."

CHAPTER 6

Sully's was an old-fashioned tavern with a scuffed-up wooden floor, oak-paneled walls, and hardwood tables and chairs. The bar itself looked like something you'd see in an old Western. The place was empty except for two men talking to the bartender, who looked to be in his early twenties.

"Can I help you folks?" the bartender asked when we'd taken stools at the bar.

"Just a couple of colas," I answered.

"You folks from out of town?" he asked as he set the sodas in front of us.

"We're staying out at the Turtle Cove Resort for the summer."

"You must be Garrett's friends. Sure is a nice thing you're doing for him. Drinks are on me."

Apparently, Garrett had told pretty much everyone on the island that we were helping him. Odd, I thought, because Garrett had left the island due to his medical issues long before I agreed to help with the project. I mentioned that to the bartender, whose name was Frank, and he informed me that Garrett was a sociable guy who kept in touch with his island family.

I guess I'd never stopped to think how hard this whole thing must have been on Garrett. I assumed he would have preferred to remain on the island for the remainder of his life, but until I got a glimpse of how integrated he was with his neighbors, I hadn't stopped to consider the fact that his leaving the island because of his stroke must be a lot harder on him than my own changing circumstance had been on me.

"Mr. Brolin from the pharmacy told me that I might be able to find Greg Norton here."

"Haven't seen him. He comes in for a cold one now and then, but usually later in the day."

"I don't suppose you know where he might be this morning. I wanted to speak to him about the town meeting on Thursday."

"Sorry, I have no idea where he is. But I can tell you one thing: the meeting is gonna be a doozy. Folks have been talkin' about it all week."

"Do you think Norton has a chance of accomplishing what he's trying to do?"

Frank paused as he dried a stack of glasses with a white bar towel. "I'd say he has a good chance. There are a lot of business owners on the island who are looking for a way to improve their bottom line. A big, fancy megaresort would make all the difference and everyone knows it."

"It sounds like you support Norton's campaign to try to force Garrett to sell to Destination Properties."

Frank shrugged. "I'm just an employee, and I really only plan to be on the island for a short time, so it won't affect me all that much one way or another, but I know Sully supports it. Change isn't always bad, you know. Times are changing and Gull Island needs to get on the bandwagon if it's going to continue to be a viable vacation spot."

I finished off the last of my cola. "Garrett doesn't want to sell."

"Norton seems to think he'll change his mind if enough folks support the idea and I tend to agree. Garrett's not going to be around anyway. I'm not sure why he even cares. Seems to me if he's in a position to help his neighbors who are struggling financially by selling his land to an organization that can make a difference, he ought to at least consider it."

"But besides Garrett's desire to keep the resort intact, there are environmental issues to consider."

"I'm not saying the environment isn't an important consideration, but at the end of the day, the human residents of the island and the economic development they depend on to thrive will find a way."

"Yes, well, I guess we'll see how it all works out. Thank you for the soda. Can you tell me the easiest way to get to the museum?"

"Just take a left when you leave the bar and then another left at the second intersection you come to. You can't miss it."

"Great, thanks. It was nice meeting you."

"So what now?" Grandpa asked as soon as we got to the car.

"I'd like to stop by the museum. Garrett recommended that we speak to a woman named Meg about the turtles as well as the history of the island. Meg was also the one to mention to the woman I met at Gertie's this morning that Norton was seen hanging around Garrett's property. I can take you back to the resort first if you'd like."

Grandpa Ben adjusted the visor above the passenger seat in an attempt to block the sun, which had shifted so that it was shining in through the windshield. "I'm game to go along. I really have nothing better to do and I've been wanting to get a look at the museum."

I started the car and pulled into traffic. The sun was high in the sky and the seagulls squawked in the distance. There was something about the smell of saltwater that filled me with a sense of contentment in spite of the turmoil rolling around in my mind.

I wanted to think that once Norton realized that Garrett had very firm plans for the resort that did not include tearing it down and building a skyscraper, he'd accept defeat and go away, but the more people I spoke to the more certain I became that that wasn't going to be the case.

"Looks like this is the place," I said as I pulled up to the curb in front of a gray stone building.

"Will you look at that view?" Grandpa Ben said as he stepped out onto the lawn.

The museum had been built on a hill, which provided an unobstructed view of the ocean in the distance. Coupled with colorful flower gardens and well-maintained walkways, the grounds provided a pleasant place to gaze out at the sea or share a snack on one of the many picnic tables.

"Welcome to the Gull Island Museum," a woman, whose nametag read MEG COLLINS, greeted us as soon as we walked in. She looked to be in her mid-sixties and had neatly styled hair in a natural silver-gray color that almost matched the lightweight blouse she wore with darker gray slacks. "How can I help you today?"

I explained who we were and what information we were interested in obtaining. Meg seemed delighted by our questions about the history of both the island and the treasure. We were the only visitors in the building, so she urged us to take seats at a table that was littered with several large photo albums and yellowed books. Once we were seated she began a narrative that was rehearsed yet informative.

"The Sea Islands," Meg began, "of which Gull Island is a part, are a chain of tidal and barrier islands off the southeastern coast of the United States reaching from South Carolina to northern Florida. Gull Island is the easternmost island in the chain, which, according to oral history, was originally settled by a group of pirates led by John Barkley in the late seventeenth century. Other islands in the area were populated by indigenous people until the Spanish began to colonize the islands in the mid-1700s."

"So if the treasure everyone is looking for belonged to a pirate who lived in the seventeenth century, it would be over three hundred years old?" I said.

"If the legend is correct, John Barkley used the island as a base of operations for several decades until he and his men were forced to head south toward the Caribbean. Unfortunately, the pirates didn't maintain a written history, nor did they keep any type of records, so what we know about their activity in this area is limited to oral history and hearsay."

"Okay, so say the fact that pirates lived on this island is true. And say there actually was a treasure. Why wouldn't Barkley take it with him when he left?"

Meg smiled. "That's where legend trumps history. As far as I know, there's no way to know exactly what Barkley did or why he did it. If we are to give credence to the legend, we'd be accepting that Barkley made the decision to leave because there were war ships in the area. It's said Barkley felt it could be difficult to protect his ill-gotten gains at sea, so he left the treasure behind with the intention of returning for it once things cooled down. According to legend, Barkley died before he made it back to this area."

"Seems like a stretch."

"I agree. Most believe, as I do, that the story of Barkley's treasure is just that: a legend. However, there were those, such as Garrett's father and grandfather, who believed very adamantly that the treasure was not only real, but is still buried somewhere on the island."

I looked down at the book I'd been thumbing through. It

was filled with maps of the islands in the area as surveyed in historical times. If the treasure did exist, and if Garrett's ancestors did indeed have a map to it, I found it hard to believe that any clues from hundreds of years ago would still make sense in terms of current landmarks.

"According to Garrett, his father and grandfather possessed a map that provided clues to the location of the treasure," I commented. "Do you happen to know where the map came from in the first place?"

"From what I've gathered, the map was discovered around a hundred years ago by Garrett's great-grandfather, who'd found the parchment sealed in a vault in one of the caverns on the island. The Hanford family was said to keep the details of the map close to their chest, so I personally have never been able to verify the authenticity of the document, if it ever existed, though I have no reason to believe their ancestors would lie about such a thing. Having said that, I'd be amazed if the map was actually left on the island by John Barkley, as Garrett's family believed."

"It would seem unlikely," I agreed.

"While I very much doubt whatever map they had belonged to John Barkley, I'd still be very much interested in obtaining it for the museum."

"According to Garrett, his mother destroyed it after his father's death."

Meg frowned.

"If a map did indeed exist, I doubt Lillabeth Hanford destroyed it. Lilly was an educated woman who would have understood the intrinsic value of a three-hundred-year-old parchment, even if it didn't actually lead to a treasure. I suppose she may have told Garrett she destroyed it as a means of preventing him from making the same mistakes his father and grandfather had. It's my guess that, if there was a map, she would have hidden it rather than destroyed it."

"So the map could very well be hidden somewhere that only a dead woman would know," I mused.

"Yes, I suppose that could be true. Such a shame. A map of that age would be a huge find for the museum."

"Or it might just bring it trouble," I pointed out. "Whether or not the map actually leads to a treasure, there are treasure hunters—quite a few, from what I've gathered—who do believe in its existence. I have a suspicion that if you were to display such an object it wouldn't take long for someone to break in and steal it."

"Yes, you could be right. It's not as if we have any sort of high-tech security system."

"Speaking of security systems, I met a woman named Bev at Gertie's Café this morning who told me that Norton had been seen loitering around Garrett's property."

"I've heard that Norton was snooping on Garrett's property from two different people," Meg confirmed. "Both are volunteers with the turtle rescue movement. One was a woman named Mamie Sue who owns a bicycle rental in town and the other is a man named Digger. He's out at the resort frequently and keeps track of all the treasure hunters in the area to make sure they don't dig too close to the nests."

"Garrett mentioned that I should tread lightly around Digger."

"He's a good man who's very passionate about the turtles, and the beach just beyond the southern border of the resort is a key nesting area," Meg informed us. "Garrett had always been good about monitoring the activity on that section of beach."

"Do you know where I can find Digger?"

"He works at the cemetery digging graves and keeping up the grounds."

"Hence the name Digger."

"Exactly. He's off on Mondays and Tuesdays, so your best

bet is to look for him on the beach. Now that nesting season is upon us, he spends most of his free time checking on the nests."

"When exactly is nesting season?"

"Early May through late August. The eggs begin to hatch in early July."

"So the eggs are close to hatching?"

"They are." Meg handed me a brochure. "I'm part of an organization that monitors and attempts to ensure the safety of as many nests and hatchlings as possible. We have teams that check on the nests every evening during hatching season."

"Do the turtles really require that much help?" Grandpa asked.

"They can use all the help they can get. Even with education programs and help from groups like ours, only about three-quarters of the eggs hatch, and only a very small percentage of the hatchlings make it to adulthood," Meg explained.

"If Mr. Norton gets his way and builds a megaresort on Garrett's land, it would impact the turtles?" I asked.

"It would be a disaster. Garrett has assured me that he'll never sell to the man, but that doesn't seem to have stopped him from trying. If he gets his way and brings all those tourists to our shores, I can guarantee you all the work we've done to protect the nests will have been for naught. One way or another, he has to be stopped."

"I intend to go to the meeting on Thursday. I'll make sure everyone knows Garrett has absolutely no intention of selling to a developer," I assured Meg.

"That's good. It appears you've arrived just in time. While there are those who are against the idea, there hasn't really been a strong opposition, if that makes any sense."

"It does. Norton is the only one with an organized campaign. I really don't see why he's bothering. He certainly can't force Garrett to sell to him."

"Garrett is a good man who will do the right thing, but I've seen instances when a great enough public need has been identified, so the courts forced a sale. It's rare, but it happens," Meg said.

"We'll just have to be sure Norton doesn't get the support he needs. The need to protect the turtles can be used as an additional argument against the sale to a developer if it should come down to that. I know one of the ski resorts in the area where I live wanted to expand and even had preliminary approval to do so until it was discovered that a rare bird had nested in the area. The ski resort had to change their plans so as not to disturb the bird."

"If it comes down to that I'll be happy to argue on behalf of the turtles."

Doc called and informed me that he'd picked up Kyle and the girls from camp since Grandpa and I had lost track of time. I hadn't meant to stay so long at the museum, but Meg was passionate about her cause and persuasive to boot. By the time we left, she had managed to obtain a promise from Grandpa to serve as a volunteer for both the museum and the Turtle League. His first turtle walk would be with Meg that very evening.

Later that afternoon I called Jenna to check in even though I'd just spoken to her on Friday. The normal cheeriness of her voice had been replaced with a tone indicating that she was tired and distressed.

"Hey, Bestie, how's it goin'?" I asked.

Jenna immediately began to cry.

"What's wrong?" I was suddenly on full alert. "Dennis? The girls? Is everyone okay?"

"Everyone is fine," Jenna sobbed. "I'm just having a bad day."

I sat down on one of the lounge chairs overlooking the sea. "Tell me everything. Start from the beginning." I had to admit I was concerned. Jenna wasn't the sort to cry at the drop of a hat.

"Everything was fine until I woke up this morning and found that Dennis hadn't come home last night."

"Hadn't come home? Surely you don't think..."

"No, I don't think Dennis is having an affair. Not with a woman at least. I do think he might be having an affair with his job."

I frowned as I tried to make sense of what Jenna was telling me. "Dennis had to work late?"

"Dennis always has to work late, and he always finds a reason to go in early. Last night he figured there was no use coming home for such a short amount of time so he stayed over with the guys."

"Dennis used to do overnight shifts all the time before his promotion," I pointed out. "You never seemed to mind."

"It was his job to stay over before. Now that he has a choice as to whether to come home or not it feels like a betrayal when he doesn't choose to spend time with me and the girls."

Okay. I could see Jenna's point. "I'm sure it won't always be this way. Dennis is new in his role as captain, and I'm sure he's just trying to let the guys know he's one of the team. I'm sure that once he settles into his new role he'll settle into a regular routine."

"I guess. But right now it's hard. Add the fact that things have been crazy at the restaurant and my best friend is AWOL and I'm just a mess."

"I'm sorry, Jen. Really. I feel like my selfish decision to come to Gull Island might very well have been a mistake with each day that goes by."

Jenna paused to blow her nose.

"No, it's not your fault. I'm just being emotional. It's been forever since Dennis and I took a vacation, which is the subject of fight number two."

"Dennis doesn't want to go on the trip you have planned?"

"He wants to postpone. He doesn't think it is the right time to be away. I guess maybe he's right, but I still feel like I've somehow become a second priority in his life behind his job."

"Come to Gull Island. We have a beautiful house right on the water with tons of extra bedrooms. You and I can visit and the girls can spend some time together."

My suggestion was met with silence.

"Jen?"

"I'm here. I'm thinking."

"Are you considering it?"

"Actually, I am. I'll have to figure out what to do about the restaurant, but the girls would love to spend some time with Ashley and Gracie. I think they feel as deserted as I do about the whole thing."

"So come."

"I'll talk to Dennis and let you know, but if I can work out the logistics, I'd love to."

CHAPTER 7

The news that Buck Barnes hadn't been murdered, as we'd assumed, but had died of natural causes came as quite a shock.

"Natural causes? But what about the head injury?" I asked Deputy Savage, who had come by the house later that evening while Grandpa and Kyle were out.

"We believe Buck hit his head when he fell." He seemed to be sincere, but my instinct told me he was lying. The problem was, his stoic facial expression and monotonous voice pattern made it impossible to know for certain.

"But he was found lying on his back and the injury was to his temple. Besides, there wasn't anything nearby for him to have hit his head on."

"I can assure you that we've taken all the evidence into account, including the placement of the body and the apparent head injury. I really can't go into detail at this time, so you'll just have to accept the fact that I've been doing this for a long time and I know what to look for. The reason I came by was to inform you that the attic is no longer off-limits. You're free to clean up as you see fit."

"Clean up? Are you sure? What if it's later determined that foul play was involved? There could be clues to be found in the attic. Fingerprints or other physical evidence, for starters."

"The death has been ruled an accident, the investigation has been closed, and Buck Barnes's body has been cremated. Like I said, you're free to clean up once I remove the tape from the attic doorway."

Deputy Savage took a step toward the stairs as if to do just that.

"Wait! This doesn't make any sense. It looked like Buck had been hit over the head and it seems like there are any number of possible suspects who might have had motive to do just that. Buck couldn't have died of natural causes. The attic was totally trashed. Someone was up there looking for something."

Deputy Savage let out a long slow breath that seemed to communicate his frustration with our conversation. "Look, I know you have good intentions, and it seems like foul play was involved, but we're certain it wasn't. Like I said, I can't tell you any more right now, but we're certain that, other than the fact that Buck obviously broke into this house, most likely to search for a map that doesn't exist, no crime has been committed. I'm going to suggest you forget all about this unfortunate incident and enjoy the rest of your summer."

Seriously?

"Now, if you'll excuse me, I really must go upstairs to remove the crime scene tape and be on my way."

There was no way Buck Barnes broke into the house, trashed the attic, had a heart attack or some other natural event that could have led to his death, and then hit his head as he fell to the floor, making it look like he'd been bludgeoned. The entire situation was ridiculous. More than ridiculous; it was downright unbelievable. And the fact that his body had been cremated was just a bit too convenient.

"What was that all about?" Doc asked after Deputy Savage left. Since both Kyle and Grandpa were out it was just the two of us with the girls.

"It seems Buck died of natural causes. The deputy came to remove the police tape from the doorway of the attic."

Doc frowned. "Natural causes? Why does he think that?"

"He declined to say. He just said they'd determined Buck died of natural causes and we were authorized to go ahead and clean up the attic."

Doc turned and headed toward the stairs without saying another word. I followed him. When we arrived at the attic he walked immediately to the place where the body had been found. "Have you been up here at all since we found the body?"

"No."

"Has anyone?"

"Just Deputy Savage. He came by on Friday night. He said he had something he wanted to check. I let him in, but he wouldn't allow me to follow him up. Why do you ask?"

"Because something is different. I can't put my finger on it at the moment, but things have been moved around. I need to take a look at the body. There's no way the injury to the head was the result of a fall."

"Savage said Buck's body has already been cremated."

"That seems convenient."

"That's what I thought. Why would the deputy rule Buck's death to be the result of some natural cause when there was obviously foul play at work? The whole thing makes no sense."

"I'm not sure." Doc walked around the attic as if he were looking for something that would explain the strange turn of events.

"Should we do something? Tell someone what we suspect?"

Doc stopped walking and turned to look at me. "If the deputy has filed a report stating that Buck died of natural causes in order to cover up a murder, which is what I suspect is going on, the coroner must be in on it as well."

"Unless the deputy never did have the coroner look at the

body," I suggested. "Remember, it was the man from the funeral home, not the coroner, who came to take the body away. Remember when Zachary died and the sheriff closed the case without even investigating? I was told that when an elderly person dies of what looks like natural causes an investigation is never opened and an autopsy isn't required. I'm not sure what the protocol is here, but if Deputy Savage is trying to cover something up, it seems that all that he had to do was exactly what he has."

Doc frowned. "It does seem as if the whole thing is being swept under the rug."

"So what do we do?"

"I'm not sure. We're new to the island and folks will have no reason to believe us if we choose to contradict what Savage is telling everyone. Without some sort of proof, it's our word against his. We'd better tread lightly."

"So we don't say anything at this point but continue to poke around on our own?"

"Exactly. You and Kyle and I were in the attic on Saturday. We can ask Kyle what he remembers when he gets back from his date, but I'm certain the attic has been tampered with. I just wish I could put my finger on exactly what it is that seems different."

"It's not a date." At least that was what I'd been trying to tell myself ever since Kyle had announced he was having dinner with Willow Rivers tonight.

I glanced at Doc, who was looking at me with a puzzled expression on his face. "Kyle's dinner with Willow," I clarified. "It's not a date. Kyle helped Willow out with a computer problem and she wanted to thank him."

"I see."

I knew Doc thought I was upset about Kyle's "not a date" because I had a thing for him, but I didn't. Kyle and I were just friends. Nothing more. More like siblings, really, in terms of our affection for each other. Kyle was free to date whoever he wanted, as was I, although the fact that he'd made plans this evening bothered me more than I'd ever admit to Doc or anyone else.

I decided to change the subject back to the cover-up. "Do you think the deputy is the one who killed Buck Barnes?"

"No. If Savage knew Barnes's remains were in the attic before we found them, he would have moved them long ago. There's something else going on, but I'm not sure what it is. I think we should have a strategy meeting after the girls go to bed. Did Ben tell you when he might be home?"

"No, but I don't think either Grandpa or Kyle planned to be out late."

"Good. I'm going to make a few phone calls while we wait for them."

I headed upstairs to begin the tucking-in process while Doc made his calls. My first stop was Gracie's room, where I found her reading a book to Pumpkin and Crissy. Both the golden retriever and the gray and white cat were snuggled up on the bed and appeared, by the look of things, to be listening intently to the story Gracie was telling.

"It looks like Pumpkin and Crissy are enjoying your story," I commented as I sat down on the edge of the bed.

"They like this book. It's one of their favorites."

I moved Gracie's hand so I could see the cover. "I remember this book. I used to read it to you."

"It's my favorite too."

"How was the kids' camp today?" Doc had ended up picking up Kyle and the girls from camp, and it had been such a hectic afternoon that I hadn't had a chance to talk to them about their day.

Gracie closed the book and set it on her bedside table. "It

was fun. I didn't want to join my group at first, so I helped Uncle Kyle with the computers, but then I made a new friend. His name is Simon."

"Wonderful. Tell me all about him."

Gracie appeared to be thinking about him. "He's nine and he's really smart. He came into the computer lab while Uncle Kyle was working and made a suggestion that Uncle Kyle thought was an excellent idea. We talked while he finished fixing the computers and then Simon and I went swimming while Uncle Kyle talked to Willow."

I adjusted my position so I could rest my back against the wall at the head of the bed. Gracie happily crawled into my arms and rested her head on my chest.

"Will Simon be there tomorrow?"

"He said yes. He lives on the island and his parents take him to camp while they're at work."

"That sounds like a good arrangement. Do you think you'll want to go to camp tomorrow?"

Gracie hesitated. "Will Uncle Kyle be there again? I heard him talking to Willow about volunteering this summer."

I tucked a lock of Gracie's hair behind her ear as I processed this bit of information. "I'm not sure what Uncle Kyle's plans are for tomorrow. We'll have to ask him, but I kind of think he was planning to return the moving van to Charleston tomorrow. Would you want to go to the camp even if he doesn't go?"

"Is Ashley going?"

"I haven't asked her yet."

"If Ash goes, I will too. Simon said he might show me the best place to catch frogs."

"That sounds like a lot of fun."

I kissed Gracie on the forehead and began to get up.

"Tj..."

"Yes, honey?"

"Do you think Papa misses us?"

Papa was what Ashley and Gracie called my dad.

"Yes, I'm sure he does."

"Do you think he's sad that we all left?"

Did I? I honestly wasn't sure. "I'm sure he misses us, but he has Rosalie with him. I think he's very happy he's living with her after all this time, and it's nice for them to have the house to themselves for a while."

"Why?"

I leaned back against the wall and pulled Gracie into my arms again. "When people first move in together they need to have time to learn how to live together as a couple. While it's possible to do that with a house full of other people, I think it's easier when the new couple have only their own needs to think about."

"What's going to happen when we go home? Will Papa and Rosalie still be learning?"

Good question.

"I wish I knew what was going to happen at the end of the summer, but I don't yet. At this point I'm just taking things a day at a time. But I want you to know that whatever happens, you and me and Ash are a family and we'll always live together. Well, at least until you're much older and want to move out on your own."

"I'm never moving away from you."

"I know that's the way you feel now, but things change when you become an adult and start to think about building a life of your own." At that moment, I couldn't believe how much the thought of Ashley and Gracie growing up and moving out someday depressed me.

"What about Grandpa? He's part of our family. Is he always going to live with us?"

"Yes, he's a part of our family, but he isn't connected to us in the same way you and me and Ashley are connected. As far as I'm concerned, he'll always be welcome to live with us unless there comes a time he doesn't want to for some reason. But I don't want you to worry about that."

"But what if you get engaged like Papa? Will you need for me and Ash and Grandpa to move so you can learn to be a couple?"

"Absolutely not. You and Ash and I are like the Three Musketeers. No one is going to come between us. I promise."

"I hope not."

I could feel Gracie's wet cheek against my chest. I held her tight while she worked through the worries caused by all the changes in her young life. In spite of the assurances everyone had been giving me, maybe dragging my sisters across the country *had* been the wrong thing to do. It had seemed to make sense at the time, but it had only been three years since our mom died and I clearly hadn't stopped to consider what upending their lives again would do to their sense of security. I held Gracie until she fell asleep, then tucked her in and headed to Ashley's room.

In contrast to Gracie's tears, Ashley actually seemed to be in a good mood. She reported that she'd also had fun at camp and had made some new friends. She definitely wanted to go back the next day and was looking forward to the movie on Wednesday. For the first time since we'd been on the island I was beginning to feel that Ashley might settle in and enjoy the summer after all.

Both Grandpa and Kyle arrived back at the house shortly after I finished tucking Ashley into bed. Kyle seemed relaxed and casual, as if his dinner with Willow really was nothing more than a meal between new friends, which I had to admit, left me with a feeling of relief.

"So we're saying Deputy Savage is for some reason lying about the fact that Buck Barnes was murdered?" Kyle clarified after we'd all settled onto the deck overlooking the ocean with glasses of wine. It was a beautiful night with a warm breeze that felt like a giant hug as it caressed my skin. The sound of nocturnal creatures rustling through the nearby shrubs competed with the soft crashing of the gentle waves, lulling me into a state of deep contentment.

"That's the way it seems," I answered as I tried to let the stress of the day evaporate into the night.

"But why?"

I shrugged. "I have no idea."

"Do you think Savage might be being bribed to close the murder investigation before it even begins?" Kyle asked.

"I hate to say it, but not all cops are good cops," Doc said. "I don't know Deputy Savage, nor have I heard anything about his reputation one way or the other, but I'd be willing to stake my own reputation as a coroner that Buck Barnes died as the result of being hit on the left temple. I did some checking while I was waiting for you and Ben to come home and I was able to ascertain that Barnes listed a man named Colin Walton as his power of attorney. It was Walton who signed off on the paperwork to have Barnes cremated."

"Who is this Colin Walton?" I wondered.

"He runs a nursing home on the island. It isn't uncommon for older folks with no next of kin to assign people like Mr. Walton the authority to make end-of-life decisions for them. From what I can gather based on the limited information I was able to obtain, Mr. Walton is very highly regarded in the community. It appears he used his own money to open the home and he makes it a point never to turn anyone away based on the inability to pay."

"Was Buck living there?" I asked.

"No, but he did odd jobs for the home, and in exchange Mr. Walton allowed Barnes to live in a small rental he owned. I think we might want to pay Mr. Walton a visit tomorrow to see if we can gain any additional insights, although, as I've already said, we'll need to tread lightly."

We fell into silence as we tried to make sense of a series of events that, when considered in their entirety, really didn't make sense. Buck Barnes seemed to be a popular fixture in the community. Everyone we'd spoken to seemed to care about the man the residents of the island seemed to have adopted. The fact that Colin Walton would agree to have him cremated without a thorough investigation seemed to indicate that he trusted Savage's conclusion regarding the cause of Barnes's death.

"I still can't believe the deputy is lying." Kyle shook his head.

"What if Deputy Savage saw something when he was in the attic that led him to the identity of the killer?" I asserted. "And what if the killer, as it turned out, was someone the deputy had a strong reason to protect?"

"Like who?" Grandpa Ben asked.

"Like a sibling or parent, perhaps even a child," I answered.

"I guess that would make sense," Grandpa agreed. "The deputy finds a clue in the attic that points to a specific person. After the body is removed, Savage comes back to clean up. Then Savage returns to say he died of natural causes, thereby eliminating the need for a thorough investigation."

"The man from the mortuary must realize Savage was lying," I pointed out. "He sees a lot of dead bodies. You'd think he'd be able to discern between those who die of natural causes and those who don't. Maybe the deputy and the man from the funeral parlor are friends. It's reasonable they would be, and I also suppose it's possible that one would cover for the other."

"If that's true I don't see how we're ever going to prove it," Kyle stated. "We really have nothing except our recollection of what we saw. It would be easy enough for a trained professional to turn around everything we think we remember so that our testimony won't hold water in court."

"Are you saying we should drop the whole thing?" I asked.

"Not at all. But I am saying that if we decide to pursue this, we're going to need to stay mindful of our limitations. We won't be helping Buck Barnes or ourselves if we end up making everyone mad."

"Sounds like we need a plan," Ben suggested.

"Sounds like we do."

Later that evening Kyle and I shared a moment of relaxation alone on the deck. It had been a really long and somewhat emotional few days, and it felt so nice just to sit and not worry about all the little things that I probably should be worrying about.

Kyle leaned back and looked up at the stars. "This is really nice. I love Paradise Lake, but there's no way we'd be sitting outside after dark without both a jacket and a fire if we were at home."

"I do like the warm nights, but I think that after a while I'd get sick of the heat. Most years by the time fall rolls around I'm ready for some snow."

"I do like having four seasons."

"I spoke to Jenna today. She is having a hard time with all the hours Dennis is putting in with his new job, so I tried to convince her to close the restaurant for a couple of weeks and come out here for a visit."

"Do you think she will?"

Echo put his head in my lap. I adjusted my position so he

would be comfortable before answering. "I think she might. It sounds like her girls miss our girls and have been giving Jenna their own sort of grief."

"Our girls?"

I smiled. "You know what I mean."

"I do. And I see why they're upset. It has to be hard when your best friend is so far away. It seems you would miss not only the friendship but the support you'd come to depend on."

"Like calling your best friend to come over and kill the spider that's crawled under your bed," I teased.

"It was a big spider!"

"It was harmless. You just pretended to be scared so I'd come over and take care of you when you were sick."

Kyle winked. "Maybe."

"Is that why you gave up everything to follow me across the country?" I asked. "Because you were afraid you'd get sick and there'd be no one around to make you soup or fluff your pillows?"

Kyle turned and looked at me with a serious expression, very much unlike the teasing I was expecting.

"I came with you because three months without you seemed intolerable."

Kyle leaned toward me just a tiny bit. I was positive he was going to kiss me. Just then, Gracie's scream pierced the silence of the night. Kyle and I both jumped up and ran into the house.

Someone must have left Blackbeard's cage open, because he was chasing Cuervo around the room, screeching, "Kill the cat, kill the cat." Cuervo was darting across furniture to avoid the sharp talons that were threatening to pierce his back, knocking everything that got in his way onto the floor.

Grandpa came running toward the sound of the chaos. "What's going on?"

"It looks like Blackbeard was really trying to kill the cat," I responded as I grabbed Blackbeard and put him back in his cage.

He chuckled as he began picking up pieces of broken glass from a vase that had crashed onto the tile floor. “Maybe we should be protecting the cat from the bird rather than the other way around.”

CHAPTER 8

Tuesday, June 20

The next morning I took Ashley and Gracie over to the kids' camp while Kyle logged onto his computer and began a search for Destination Properties. Kyle had inherited a lot of money a couple of years earlier and no longer needed to work, but prior to his inheritance he'd been a software developer, and a good one at that. He knew his way around a computer and the internet. In the past, I'd learned to trust that whenever we really needed a piece of information, Kyle would find a way to get it.

"What did you find?" I asked after I returned from my errand.

Kyle sat at a desk that held his laptop. He leaned back in his chair and looked at me. "On the surface, Destination Properties is a legitimate company. It owns resort properties in most of the Caribbean, Mexico, and Central and South America. Most of their places are the all-inclusive kind that provide vacationers with stress-free trips where everything is paid for and taken care of ahead of time. They're fairly high end and seem to attract a more affluent clientele."

"Okay, so why would a huge company like that even be interested in Garrett's little piece of land?"

"My sense is that the company wants to expand into properties within the United States. Based on my research, they were looking at a location in Florida that didn't pan out, so they turned their sights to Gull Island. Garrett's property is actually larger than you'd think based on the buildings contained on the resort." Kyle pulled up a map. "If you look at the property lines on record, the land Garrett owns includes this entire part of the island." Kyle drew a circle with his finger.

"Wow. I had no idea."

"If a large company with deep pockets got hold of the property my sense is that most of this land, which at this point has been left natural, would be developed."

"Which would be catastrophic for the wildlife that live here," I said.

"It would seem so."

I already knew I wanted to stop Norton in his campaign to force Garrett to sell his property to Destination Properties; now I just had to figure out how I could use this new information to my advantage. "Bev said the company was known for buying distressed properties, and her opinion was that Destination Properties was responsible for causing the problems in the first place. I wonder if Norton has plans to sabotage Turtle Cove."

"I wouldn't be surprised if that were the case. I found a property in Mexico that Destination Properties had its eye on. The owner wanted top dollar because there was existing infrastructure that could be used for lodging. Destination Properties insisted they weren't willing to pay for the buildings because they didn't plan to use them and were interested in the land only. The property owner decided to look elsewhere for a buyer and received another offer, but there was a fire and the main structure burned to the ground. The owner had been in trouble financially prior to putting the property up for sale and had let the insurance lapse. The new buyer wasn't interested in the property without the lodging facility and Destination Properties ended up buying the land for less than their original offer."

"Sounds suspicious."

"There's more. I found an instance where Destination Properties had arranged to buy a piece of oceanfront property in the Bahamas, but before the deal was finalized it was discovered there had been a chemical spill on the grounds. The owner couldn't afford to have the spill cleaned up, and there are very few buyers who are willing to take on such a liability, so the property ended up selling to Destination Properties for a fraction of their original offer. Of course," Kyle qualified, "there's no way to prove these things weren't simply coincidences, though I'd be surprised if they were."

I sat back and looked out the window. I couldn't help but remember my theory that perhaps Buck had been out at Garrett's house looking for the map when he saw something he shouldn't have. Was it possible Buck had run into Norton while he was tampering with the property in some way so as to assure that he'd end up winning the bid to buy the land? I hadn't noticed anything odd from a cursory look, but it seemed prudent that we took a closer look around.

"I'm beginning to think that Buck's death and Norton's bid to buy Garrett's land are linked in some way, but I really have no way to prove it."

"I'll keep looking," Kyle offered. "If we can find enough instances where Destination Properties just happened to buy a valuable piece of land for pennies on the dollar due to some sort of an unfortunate incident, maybe we can make a strong enough case for people to stop and take notice."

Kyle went back to his search for additional case studies to

use against Destination Properties while I went into the kitchen for some coffee. I had several goals for the day. The first was what Kyle was working on, finding out what he could about Destination Properties in the hope of coming up with ammunition I could use against Greg Norton and his campaign to take Garrett's land; the other was to refine my suspect list by speaking to anyone I could, and hopefully narrowing the pool. There was no way I was prepared to believe the deputy's assertion that Buck had died of natural causes in spite of how much everyone we talked to seemed to love the guy.

I took out my notebook and considered the entries. I currently had Toby Upton in the yellow zone. I hadn't had a chance to speak to either Adam or Beth Joyner, so I'd yet to add a color to their names. Greg Norton was firmly in the red zone until I could prove otherwise. I hated to do it, but ever since Deputy Savage had announced that Buck's case was closed I had to consider him a suspect, so I added Savage to the yellow zone as well. If he'd been the one to kill Buck himself, he would most likely have had the presence of mind to move the body long before we arrived on the island, but I couldn't help but feel he was covering for whoever had, which made him a suspect of sorts.

I'd also added a column for people I wanted to interview. Meg had originally been on the list, but now that I'd spoken to her I crossed her off and added Mamie Sue and Digger. Meg mentioned that Digger was off work on Mondays and Tuesdays, so unless I happened to run into him on the beach my talk with him would need to wait. I remembered that Mamie Sue owned a shop that rented bikes, so I called Gertie and asked for directions and then headed into town to see what, if anything, I could find out about Norton's presence on Garrett's property.

Once I arrived at my destination I let myself into the colorfully decorated shop and walked up to the rental counter.

"Mamie Sue, my name is..."

"Tj," the buxom blond with big hair finished. "Gertie told me you were coming by. Aren't you just the cutest little thing this side of the Mississippi?"

I wasn't sure how to respond to that, so I just got right to my question. "I met with Meg from the museum yesterday and she told me that you had seen Greg Norton snooping around on Garrett's property."

"I surely did. Talk about a rooster in the hen house. The man is going around telling everyone about all the good his company is going to bring to the island in spite of the significant damage his resort will do to the native turtle population. Those of us who belong to the Turtle League have tried to convey to the area's population just how catastrophic to the environment a resort such as the one Destination Properties plans to build will be. Norton has done a passable job countering our argument with rhetoric while secretly working to sabotage this year's eggs."

"He's been damaging the eggs?"

"Moving them. His claim is that the turtles have found other nesting grounds and will eventually stop laying eggs on the beach at Turtle Cove all together as evidenced by the sharp decrease in numbers being reported by volunteers this year. I had a feeling that man was up to no good, but Norton did seem to have the math to back up his claims. There have been less eggs. I thought we might be in trouble until I caught the man in the act of bagging up the eggs. I swear the man backpedaled all the way to the Mason Dixon line when I threatened to call the sheriff."

"Did you?"

"I did, but Mr. Norton's fancy attorney managed to convince the man that I was mistaken in what I'd seen. Unfortunately, I didn't have any evidence to support my claim. I told Digger what I'd seen and he promised to take care of the man once and for all."

If Norton had been my victim, I would assume that taking care of things was exactly what Digger had done, but I still didn't see why Digger would kill Buck. I asked Mamie Sue if she knew where I could find Digger, but she reported that he was out on his boat and wouldn't be back until the following day. I decided to track down the next name on my list, Adam Joyner. Chances were if he was working with Buck prior to his death he could provide me with something useful about his activities during that time period. I called Kyle and let him know what I was doing. Hopefully he and I would both have come up with useful information by the time we met for lunch in a couple of hours.

The post office was in the center of the downtown district, which was really just a few square blocks where all the shops and businesses were located. I walked in to find a man behind the counter looking into a box in front of him, along with Deputy Savage, who was standing on the customer side. I walked up beside Deputy Savage and looked into the box as well.

"Kittens," I said with a smile. I looked at the deputy. "Are they yours?"

"No. I'm more of a dog person myself."

"I found the box with the kittens at the back door near the loading dock," the man behind the counter explained. "The post office doesn't deal with the delivery of livestock, so I called Deputy Savage."

I frowned. "Who would mail kittens?"

Savage turned the box so I could see the address. "Santa Claus, North Pole" had been written in crayon, and the only return address was a hand-drawn picture of a house with a tree beside it. "I don't suppose you're in the market for a kitten?" Savage asked me.

I looked at the four little furballs. "They're adorable, but I'm afraid our household already consists of four cats, three dogs, and a parrot. What will happen to them?"

"I'll make sure they're either returned to their adult owner, if one can be found, or adopted into good homes," Savage promised. The deputy looked at the man behind the counter. "I should be going. Call me if anyone comes around looking for the little darlings."

I watched as the tall deputy picked up the box and headed out the front door.

"You don't have an animal shelter on the island?" I wondered.

"'Fraid not. Don't worry though; Rick will make sure the kittens are well taken care of."

"Has he done this kind of thing before?" I turned and stared at the door Deputy Savage had just gone through. "Taken responsibility for stray and abandoned animals?"

"Many times. Now, how can I help you?"

I looked at the man, who had the name "Adam Joyner" embroidered on his shirt. "I'm staying out at Garrett Hanford's place for the summer and I wanted to be sure you had my name, as well as the names of the others who will be with me, should we receive mail sent in care of the resort."

Adam handed me a form. "Fill this out."

"I'm really enjoying my stay in your town," I said to him as I began to fill out the form. "The locals are all so nice. I feel right at home."

"Gull Island is the home of a lot of nice folks."

"I've really found that to be true. I guess you heard about Buck Barnes. Pretty much everyone I've met has been so helpful in trying to help me understand what happened to that poor man."

Joyner gave me an odd look.

"Doesn't seem like it would really be your problem to understand a matter like that."

I paused in my writing and looked up at him. "I suppose that's true, but considering I'm the one who found the body, I guess I'm just curious. Seems that most people in town were really fond of Buck, although I've found a few exceptions."

"Buck was a good guy," Adam assured me. "A bit of a dreamer, but a good guy."

I slid the completed form across the counter. "I heard he was onto a treasure before he passed. I find the whole thing very interesting."

"You into treasure hunting?" he asked as he entered the information I'd given him into the computer.

"No, I can't say I've ever been involved in a treasure hunt, but I imagine it would be a fascinating thing to do."

"Fascinating, maybe, but the end of the rainbow can be as much of a disappointment as the map that leads you there. I think I have everything I need to ensure that you get your mail while you're on the island."

"Thank you. I appreciate that." I turned and then moved back to the counter. "You must know everyone in town, given the job you do. I don't suppose you know might know the identity of two men that had been seen with Buck prior to his disappearance?"

Adam frowned. "Why are you looking for them?"

"I'm just curious. Besides I heard that there are some people who think your wife could be a suspect, but my money is on the two strangers."

I watched a myriad of emotions cross Adam's face. "What do you mean my wife is a suspect? Beth wouldn't hurt a fly."

"That's not what I heard. I've been told that when she found out you'd joined Buck in his treasure hunt she threatened to hit him upside the head."

"Sure, she was mad. She had every right to be. But Beth didn't kill anyone. She had no reason to."

"Unless I've been given false information and you're actually the one who funded the project. Spouses have been known to become quite violent when money is involved."

Adam shook his head. "Buck was looking for a backer for his treasure hunt, but it wasn't me who gave Buck the money he needed, although he could be a convincing salesman. He told me he got the money he needed form another source, but still needed help with the actual dig. Somehow he talked me into taking a leave of absence from the post office. Buck assured me he had a way to get the map and knew where to find the treasure. He seemed to know stuff only someone who had actually seen the map would know, and I got caught up in the moment. But I didn't kill him or harm him in any way, and neither did Beth. I really liked the guy. He used to sweep up here two days a week and we'd chat."

"Do you think he tried to con you?"

"Buck? No. He really believed he had a way to get the map. I'd stake what's left of my reputation on it."

"So if you didn't fund the project, who did?"

"The two men you asked about. Buck referred to them as Dilly and Lambert. Those are the only names I know."

"Do you know where I can find them?"

Adam wrote down an address in Charleston. "I'd be careful if I were you. Those men didn't seem to me to be the type who would welcome an interrogation."

"Thanks." I took the piece of paper and put it in my pocket. "I'll keep that in mind."

As I left the post office I took out my notebook and changed Deputy Savage's name on my suspect list to green, my code for likely innocence. I didn't know why he was trying to cover up the murder, or even if that was what he was really trying to do, but anyone who would take a box of abandoned kittens home didn't strike me as a cold-blooded killer. Besides, Doc had a good point that if Savage was the killer he would have removed Buck's body from the attic long before we arrived.

Adam seemed innocent as well, and I was willing to bet his wife was too, which left me with Dilly and Lambert and Greg Norton.

I still thought that Norton was my best suspect, but I figured it wouldn't hurt to have a conversation with Dilly and Lambert. We did still need to return the rental van, so I called Kyle and suggested that the two of us take a trip to Charleston. It was only an hour's drive, so we'd have plenty of time to return the van and look up Dilly and Lambert before it was time to pick up the girls from kids' camp. Just to be on the safe side. However, I arranged for Doc to fetch them if Kyle and I were held up for some reason.

Charleston was a charming city filled with romance and history. The horse-drawn carriages and brick buildings that had stood the test of time grabbed me from the very first moment I saw them. This summer's trip was my first to this part of the country, and if I'd known what I'd been missing, I would have come east much sooner. As we drove through the busy streets I couldn't help but let my imagination wander to a simpler time when the city had first been built.

"I know we're in a hurry today, but we have to come back and do the tourist things here," I said to Kyle after he dropped off the van and joined me in my car to look for the address Adam Joyner had given me.

"It really is charming. We should bring the girls to the aquarium. I hear they have a turtle hospital you can visit."

"Sounds like fun. I'd love to spend a day walking around the old town. It looks as if there's a lot of history just waiting to be soaked up."

"There're a lot of historical sites to see up and down the coast. Maybe we can take a road trip at some point this summer."

"Sounds great," I said, looking out the window. "I think we need to take a left at the next stoplight." Thank goodness for cell phones with map apps. I couldn't imagine trying to navigate my way around such a large city without one. Back home at Paradise Lake things were pretty easy to find because there was only one main road that encircled the lake.

"Do we know what this address is to?" Kyle asked. "Dilly's home? Lambert's? A place of business?"

"I'm not sure," I admitted. "I guess I should have gotten more information. I've really been off my game lately, forgetting to ask all the questions I should during this investigation. I suppose I could call Adam Joyner. The number for the post office on Gull Island should be listed."

"Let's see what we find when we reach the destination and then we can decide," Kyle suggested. "Do we know anything at all about these men other than that they seemed to have been working with Buck?"

I glanced at Kyle. "No."

"We had to come to Charleston to return the van anyway, and I don't suppose there's any harm in driving past the address, but if things look hinky at all we're going to head straight back to Gull Island and do some more research before we start knocking on doors in a strange city."

"Agreed."

The address Adam had given me was to a townhouse in a decent, if not upscale, neighborhood. I wasn't sure who lived there, but Kyle and I decided it looked innocent enough for us to knock on the door and see what happened. Kyle parked the car along the curb and we both walked up the paved walkway to the ground-floor unit. We knocked once and a teenage girl answered the door.

"Can I help you?"

"Hi. My name is Tj Jensen, and this is Kyle Donovan. This is going to sound a little odd, but we're are looking for two men named Dilly and Lambert. We understand one of them lives here."

The girl looked at us suspiciously. "Who are you exactly?"

"Friends of someone the men used to know," I said, stretching the truth somewhat.

Kyle smiled at the girl. "I'm sure this sounds strange, but we just want to speak to them."

The girl shrugged. "My uncle's last name is Lambert. He owns this townhouse. He's out of the country, so my mom and I are staying here. He'll be back on Friday. I can leave a message if you'd like."

"I would. Thank you." I took out my notebook and turned to a clean page. I wrote down my name and cell number and handed it to the girl. "And the other man, Dilly? Do you know where we can find him?"

"Dilly lives on Folly Island. I'm not sure of his address, but everyone there knows him. If you want to find him just ask around."

We thanked her and returned to the car. "What do you think?" I asked. "Folly Island isn't that far out of our way."

Kyle shrugged. "I don't see why not. We should call Doc though and let him know he should plan to pick the girls up from camp."

The drive from Charleston to Folly Island took less than an hour even with traffic. When we arrived we decided to grab a bite to eat while we fished around for information about Dilly. I had assumed Dilly and Lambert were friends who lived in close proximity to each other, but it appeared they lived a good thirty miles apart.

We ordered roast beef sandwiches at a small café and asked the waitress if she knew where we could find Dilly, and she gave us the address of a local bar where he liked to hang out.

CHAPTER 9

"The man at the bar down the street said to look for a man with long blond hair wearing a ratty old Yankees cap," I whispered to Kyle as we entered the third bar in our attempt to track down Dilly.

Kyle tilted his head across the floor. "Looks like that could be him over there, playing pool."

"Let's just walk up and pretend we've met before and see what happens," I suggested.

"I'll follow your lead."

I walked across the bar with Kyle walking closely behind me. "Dilly," I said when I arrived at the table. "It's Tj," I added when he just stared at me. "From Gull Island," I specified when he still didn't respond.

He still looked confused, but he replied, "Oh, Tj. How are you?"

"Good. And yourself?"

"Hangin' in there."

"I didn't realize you lived on Folly Island. It's a great place, but for some reason I thought both you and Lambert lived in Charleston."

"I did live there at one time, but I like to move around."

Dilly had an odd look on his face. He was probably trying to place me while maintaining the conversation at the same time.

"I guess you heard about Buck."

The man narrowed his gaze. "Yeah. What of it?"

"There's a rumor going around that you might know something about his death."

"Who's saying that?"

I looked around the room. It wasn't crowded, but this didn't seem like the type of conversation to have at a pool table. "How about my friend and I buy you a drink?" I nodded toward an empty table in the corner.

"You a cop?"

"No, I'm not a cop. I heard some people say that you were considered a suspect in Buck's murder, and when I saw you standing here, I figured the friendly thing would be to give you a heads up."

"That is mighty neighborly, and I guess I could use a drink."

I led Dilly over to the table while Kyle went up to the bar and ordered drinks for all three of us.

"Where do I know you from again?" Dilly was beginning to look even more confused.

"Sully's. I'm not surprised you're having a hard time remembering. You were pretty smashed the night we met. In fact, we were both pretty smashed."

"Yeah, I guess I remember you now."

"You were in the bar with Lambert and the three of us partied. I had a really good time, so when I was in Charleston today I stopped by Lambert's place to say hi, but I guess he's still out of the country."

"Yeah. You know how it is with those tech guys. Always traveling."

"I know what you mean. Based on what he said, it seems like he's pretty swamped." I knew I was laying on the lie pretty thick; I just hoped it wasn't too thick. "I'm kind of surprised he took the time to come to Gull Island with you in the first place."

"Lambert and I are friends from way back. We took different paths, but we still try to get together every now and then. He calls me his vacation-from-reality buddy. When we get together we do stuff he'd never do in his regular life."

"Like go on a treasure hunt?"

"Yeah. 'Course, the treasure hunt Buck took us on was a fake. I'm pretty sure there never was a map. I felt kind of bad for talking Lambert into giving him all that money. Not that he can't afford it. He just got a new job working with Apple."

Kyle returned to the table and set down the glasses he was carrying in the middle of the hardwood surface. "I work in the software industry. I wonder if I know your friend."

"Might. Daryl is really smart. He even developed a game a while back. He didn't make a lot of money off of it, but it was pretty awesome."

"I'd love to check it out sometime. Maybe when Lambert returns from his trip."

"I got a copy if you want to check it out," Dilly offered. "I live just down the street."

"I'd like that." Kyle smiled.

Dilly had obviously been drinking and I wasn't thrilled about going to his house, but I wasn't alone and I guess it wouldn't hurt to take a look around and see if anything stood out as suspicious.

"We can just walk if you want," Dilly suggested. "It's really close."

"Sounds good to me," I answered.

Dilly chugged his beer before he got up from the table, waved to the bartender, and led us out of the building.

"So how long has Lambert been out of the country?" I asked as we made our way down the street.

"Long time. He left on May 15th, right after our trip to Gull Island. He should be back in a couple weeks."

If that were true then Lambert at least couldn't be the killer since, based on the timeline I'd put together, Buck had only been missing since May 30th.

"I know you said that Lambert does computer stuff. What do you do for a living?" I asked.

"Little of this, little of that. Right now I'm between jobs, but I just got back from visiting my cousin in Kansas. He gave me five grand to help him build a room onto his house. Not bad for a month's work. Here we are." Dilly stopped in front of a dilapidated old house. "It's not much, but it's home."

Dilly's house was old and rundown. The moment he opened the door I was hit with the stench of alcohol and rotting food. I really did want to solve Buck's murder, but it sounded as if Dilly and Lambert were both out of town when Buck was killed, so if their alibis checked out, they couldn't be the killer we were looking for anyway.

"You know," I said as the overwhelming urge to gag overtook me, "I think I'll just wait out here in the fresh air. I'm afraid I might be allergic to something in your house."

Dilly shrugged. "Suit yourself." He turned to look at Kyle. "You coming?"

Kyle glanced at me with a look of resignation on his face. "I'd love to take a quick look at what you have, although we can't stay long."

"Just a few minutes," I warned, "or we'll be late for that appointment we really shouldn't be late for."

By the time Kyle and I returned from Charleston, Doc had picked up the girls from camp. I prepared a light dinner for the others, after which Kyle and I tried to decide on our next move in what I was beginning to refer to as *our* murder case. I had to admit I was beginning to feel torn. Part of me felt I should be putting all my energy into trying to stop Greg Norton and Destination Properties' plans, while another wanted to put all my efforts into figuring out what had happened to Buck. I supposed that until the renovation of the resort got underway I could try to do both.

In terms of the murder investigation I had two pressing questions: who had killed Buck and why the deputy was lying to cover up the fact that Buck's death really had been a murder. Grandpa had been at the museum with Meg that day and he'd broached the subject of Deputy Savage's reputation in the community. Meg had assured him the man was not only well liked but was a respected law enforcement officer who spent a good deal of his spare time volunteering for various organizations on the island.

After dinner was over and the dishes had been washed and put away, I settled the girls in front of the television so Kyle, Doc, Grandpa, and I could discuss the first matter at hand, which, as it turned out, revolved around the deputy.

"If we're going to operate on the assumption that Deputy Savage knows who murdered Buck and is indeed covering up the murder, maybe the key to this whole thing is in figuring out who it is the deputy cares enough about to lie for," Kyle suggested. "Is Savage married?"

"Meg said he's single and childless, although he does have siblings: two brothers and a sister. One of the brothers and the sister live on the island and the other brother lives in Charleston," Grandpa reported.

"Do you think Meg found it odd that you were asking all these personal questions about Deputy Savage?"

"No, because I didn't just ask about him. It was slow at the museum today, so I took advantage of the downtime to ask about pretty much everyone I've met since I've been here." My grandfather looked at Kyle. "Did you know Willow has a daughter?"

"Yeah, she introduced us. Cute little thing. Her dad is out of the picture, so Willow is raising her alone, although I have a feeling she might have her eye on someone to take on the dad role."

"Do you know who that is?" I had to ask.

"She didn't say and I don't know her well enough to ask. You know, there's a boy at the kids' camp named Rory Savage. I wonder if he's any relation to the good deputy."

"Rory is his nephew," Grandpa confirmed. "Deputy Savage's brother has three children. The deputy coaches Rory's baseball team."

I wondered where Savage found the time to do so much volunteer work and said as much to the others.

"Meg commented that most of the time there isn't a lot of crime to deal with on the island. I guess the low crime rate allows him to multitask. She made a joke about the fact that he's been known to show up at a crime scene wearing his softball uniform."

"You really did manage to dig up quite a bit of information in just a couple of hours," I said.

"Meg likes to talk, and I was motivated to listen. The thing is, the more she talked about Savage, the more certain I became that if he's covering up a murder he must have a really good reason to do it. He seems like an all-around good guy."

"Yeah, something isn't jiving." I looked at Doc. "Are you sure the damage to the skull couldn't have occurred as the result of a fall?"

"I'm sure."

"Okay." I looked around the table. "Now that we have all this new information, where do we start?"

"I talked to Meg some more about this Norton fellow," my grandfather said. "She suggested that you might want to have a discussion with the mayor prior to Thursday's meeting."

"Okay. Who is the mayor?"

"A woman named Betty Sue Bell. Meg said she owns Betty Boop's, a hair salon on Cove Street."

"The contractor is coming by in the morning, but I'll go by after that to see what she has to say about this whole thing."

"Contractor?" Ben asked.

"A man by the name of Jack Long. When I spoke to Garrett just before we left to head east he mentioned that Jack would be stopping by on the morning of the twenty-first to discuss what needs to be done. It seems the two of them have already had a preliminary conversation, but Garrett indicated that Jack wanted to do a complete inventory of the existing infrastructure before they settled on a plan."

"Makes sense. I took a walk around today and couldn't help but notice that a few of the cabins are in really bad shape."

We ironed out the details for the following day and then both Grandpa Ben and Doc headed into the house, while Kyle and I retired to the deck with glasses of wine. It really was a beautiful evening. The moon was shining on the water, creating a serene environment.

"Don't let me forget to tuck Blackbeard in before we head in for the night," Kyle said.

"Blackbeard asked about you this morning. I think he might have a little birdie crush," I teased.

"He asked about me?"

"When I went in to feed him, he repeatedly asked for Captain Kyle."

"I know parrots are supposed to simply mimic what they hear, but I swear, that bird has a mind of its own, although the Captain Kyle thing came from Gracie."

I laughed. “Were you playing pirate again?”

Kyle blushed. “When we got home from camp yesterday I decided to take the dogs for a walk. Gracie wanted to go and she asked if we could bring Blackbeard. I found a tether that goes around his leg so you can take him outdoors and not worry about him flying away, so I agreed to take him. When I opened the door to the cage he said, ‘Play with pretty boy,’ and Gracie told him my name was Captain Kyle. He called me Captain Kyle for the entire walk. I’m not sure he has a crush on me though. He told me to walk the plank several times during the twenty minutes we were on the beach.”

“That’s funny. Garrett must watch pirate movies. Either that or he plays pirate with Blackbeard as well. It’s really amazing the way he seems to really be talking to us and not just repeating random words.”

“He actually has a pretty large vocabulary.”

“When I was a kid I had a friend with a parrot. The bird’s name was Rodney. Rodney could talk, but it never felt like he was communicating. To be honest I remember thinking the bird was a pest. He was loud and messy and I really couldn’t understand why anyone would want to own such a creature. But Blackbeard is different. If you told me that Blackbeard was really a handsome prince who had a spell cast on him turning him into a bird, I’d totally buy it.”

“Why is it that all the stories about people being turned into animals involved handsome princes?” Kyle wondered.

“I guess so the beautiful princess will have a strong enough motive to want to kiss a hundred frogs trying to find the right one. Personally, the prince would have to have a lot more going on for him than just being handsome for me to kiss a pond full of frogs.”

Kyle laughed. “Oh, and what qualities would this fairytale prince need to possess to get your attention?”

I took a sip of my wine and leaned back in my chair. “If I was going to kiss a frog to free a prince, I’d want the prince to be someone who was capable of being a partner in life and not just arm candy. He’d need to care about me and my sisters and he’d need to be interested in becoming part of a readymade family and not just riding off into the sunset with the beautiful princess. He’d have to love animals, have a good sense of humor, and embrace everyday moments like the first snow or a perfect sunset. He’d need to be open to possibilities and he’d need to find magic in the little things like stolen kisses and fuzzy mittens. And most of all, he’d need to have a kind heart and gentle spirit.”

“Anything else?”

“He’d need to be loyal and trustworthy like a dog, but a better kisser.”

“Sounds like you’ve thought about this.”

I frowned. “Yeah. I guess I have.” I turned my head to the side so I was looking directly at Kyle. “The thing is, that even if you find Prince Charming and he’s everything that you ever thought you’d want, sometimes that isn’t enough. My grandmother used to say that love isn’t logical, that sometimes you just have to trust your heart to find the other half of itself.”

Kyle leaned in until his lips were only inches from mine. “How will you know?”

“You’ll know.”

CHAPTER 10

Wednesday, June 21

When Jack Long arrived the next morning in his faded blue jeans, tight blue t-shirt, smoky gray eyes, and dark blond hair, I knew for certain that Kyle's almost kiss had affected me more than I wanted to admit. Not only had I dreamed about that moment for most of the night, but Jack was exactly my type, yet I found I felt nothing when he smiled at me with his sexy grin or winked at me. Maybe Jenna was right. Maybe Kyle was the one I'd been waiting for. If Gracie hadn't interrupted us at the exact moment of our almost kiss, maybe I'd know for sure whether or not it would be Kyle's kiss that would break the curse and wake the dormant half of my heart.

"Ms. Jensen?"

"You can call me Tj." I forced my attention back to the matter at hand. "I know you've spoken to Garrett and have a general idea as to what needs to be done."

"We had a dialogue about the project, but I wanted to get a look at the place before I made my recommendations. Do you happen to know if the cabins are locked?"

"They are. Just let me get the keys and I'll show you around."

"Thanks. I'd appreciate it. Are you enjoying island life so far?"

All three dogs wandered over to check out the visitor. Echo stayed by my side, but Trooper and Pumpkin went in for the scratch behind the ears, which Jack seemed happy to provide.

"It's a beautiful place, and in spite of the body we discovered in the attic on the day we arrived, I've enjoyed my time here very much so far."

"I heard you stumbled on old Buck. It's a shame what happened to him. He was an odd sort, but a nicer guy you wouldn't find."

"Odd?" I asked as I opened the side door and let myself into the kitchen, where the keys were located in a cabinet.

"Maybe odd isn't the right word. The guy was friendlier than most, but at times he appeared to be a bit too friendly, if you know what I mean."

"Too friendly?" I found the keys we would need and we headed back out into the warm sunshine. I was beginning to see a pattern. Almost every person I'd spoken to had described Buck as too friendly.

"For example, we had a big scare last summer when Buck struck up a conversation with a four-year-old he came across while he was walking down the street. The carnival was in town and the child was crying because his mom said she was too busy to take him. Buck felt bad for the kid, so he offered to accompany him and even pay for the rides. The problem was that he didn't think to inform the child's mother of his intention. When she went outside to look for her son and couldn't find him, she thought he'd been kidnapped. Luckily, he was found safe and sound at the carnival with Buck, but only after half the island had dropped everything to look for him."

"Yikes."

"Yikes is right. The woman was a visitor and wanted to charge Buck with kidnapping, but Deputy Savage managed to talk her out of it. He also had a long talk with Buck, who seemed to understand what he'd done wrong. At least, he hadn't taken off with any more kids that I know of."

I would die if Ashley or Gracie disappeared, but I could see where a simple man would think he was doing a nice thing by taking the child to the carnival when his mother couldn't.

"It seems the locals all pitched in to take care of Buck."

"That's mostly true, although there were a few who didn't see eye to eye with him. Generally speaking, we like to take care of our own around here, and Buck was one of us, no matter his limitations. Garrett too. That's why I want to be sure we come up with a plan that will help ensure that Garrett's desires concerning the resort are met to the best of our abilities."

I was liking this guy more and more. It turned out that not only was Jack Long very good-looking, he was also knowledgeable about the renovation processes, and funny and friendly to boot.

"The main problem I see is we need to make the necessary repairs that will attract a buyer who'll be interested in maintaining the integrity of the resort without spending so much on the project that any interested party would never be able to afford the price Garrett would need to charge to recover his investment."

"Do you have any idea why Garrett let the property slide into such a state of disrepair?" I asked.

"I think the decay occurred over time. When you're around something every day you tend not to notice that the floors need refinishing and the exterior of the cabins have begun to deteriorate. Garrett had medical issues even before his stroke and the maintenance must have gotten to be too much for him.

He should have hired someone to keep the place up years ago, but he'd always been a hands-on guy who probably convinced himself that just because he wasn't up to a big project one year he might be the next, so he put it on the back burner."

I looked around at everything I could see. The property itself was spectacular, but Jack was correct that the structures were going to need a lot of work, maybe more than Garrett could afford.

"I guess you've heard that Destination Properties has launched a campaign to try to pressure Garrett into selling so they can build a megaresort on the property."

"I've heard. To be honest I'd hate to see him sell to Destination Properties, but from a financial standpoint it makes a lot of sense."

"Have you discussed this with Garrett?"

"Actually, I have. He's adamant that he isn't going to sell to the company, so I agreed to help him with this project, although I do think it's important to do the renovations as inexpensively as possible just in case."

"Just in case of what?"

"Just in case Greg Norton gets his way. He doesn't strike me as the type to take no for an answer."

"What are you going to suggest to Garrett?"

"I'm not sure. It almost makes the most sense to tear down the cabins in the worst condition and focus on the ones that require less work. Fewer cabins in good repair could actually prove to be more marketable than more cabins in a state of disrepair. The thing I'm uncertain about is how many cabins are necessary to make the cash flow work from a rental standpoint. Garrett might be better off subdividing the land and selling the cabins off individually rather than trying to sell the property as a resort. If he wants to protect the integrity of the land, he's going to have a hard time finding a buyer who's willing to maintain the rustic feel of the place and yet can afford to purchase the whole enchilada. I'd like to take a few days to draw up a plan for Garrett to consider before we begin work."

I shrugged. "It's okay with me if it's okay with Garrett. I have another project I'm working on anyway."

"Great. I'm going to take some measurements and make some notes, then I'll call Garrett this afternoon. I should be able to have something to him by next week."

"Sounds good." I decided to walk Jack back to his truck, which was filled with baseball equipment. "You coach baseball?"

"I play softball."

"They have an adult league on the island?"

"We have an adult *team* on the island. We play teams from other islands. You don't play, do you?"

"I have. In fact, I coach the girls' softball team at the high school where I teach."

"Really? I don't suppose you'd be interested in filling in for a tournament we're playing in the weekend after next? One of our regulars is about to have a baby, so we're short a player."

"The tournament is on Gull Island?"

"At the recreation center on Shell Beach," Jack confirmed.

"Okay, I'm in. It sounds like fun. What time do you need me to be there?"

"Nine a.m. on Saturday, July 2nd. We're having a couple of practices between now and then, if you can make them. It'll give you a chance to meet everyone before the tournament."

"I'll try. When is the next practice?"

"Friday at six."

"Great. I'll see you then."

"You'll need a team hat and shirt. I'll let Rick Savage know. He's the team manager. You can just pick them up at practice."

I felt a little odd about playing softball with the man I secretly suspected of covering up a murder, but I'd already told

Jack I'd do it and I didn't want to back out now. I wondered how Deputy Savage was going to take the news that I was his new teammate. If he was lying—and my sense was that he was—he had to realize I wasn't buying everything he was telling me.

"The pharmacist called earlier," Grandpa Ben announced after Jack had left and he'd returned from his walk. "He needs me to sign a release I missed when we were there before. If you want to give me a ride we can stop by Betty Boop's after."

"I'd be happy to. Oh, and tonight is the movie on the beach. I promised the girls we'd go, so we should be sure to be back home in time for an early dinner."

"Meg said there are food trucks there, and most folks just bring a blanket and eat on the beach."

"Even better. I have to admit I'm almost as excited about the movie as the girls are. There's something magical about the idea of watching a movie under the stars."

"When Gertie mentioned it, I remembered that drive-in we used to go to when you were a kid."

"I thought about that too." I smiled. "I have such fond memories of those summer nights. It's too bad the drive-in shut down. It would be fun to take the girls."

"Might want to suggest an outdoor movie night to your dad. It would be a fun event for Maggie's Hideaway to sponsor."

"Yeah, I'll do that. Have you talked to Dad since we've been here?"

"I thought about calling, but I figured the whole purpose of this trip was to give him and Rosalie some space. Besides, I'm sure it's starting to get busy at the resort, so I hate to bother him."

"Last night Gracie asked me what was going to happen when we went home and I realized I really had no idea."

"You know your dad is happy to have you and the girls at the resort."

"I know. And Rosalie has told me on more than one occasion that she's fine with it as well. I can't help but wonder though if they don't secretly wish they didn't have a house full of people underfoot all the time."

"I know how you feel. Doc offered to have me move in with him."

"Are you going to?"

Grandpa frowned. "I'm not sure. Doc and I get along and he has a big house, but I think I'd miss making breakfast for the girls in the mornings and hearing about their day when they get home from school."

"We have time to figure it out. Let's go ahead and head into town."

As soon as we arrived at the pharmacy, my grandfather signed the paperwork, then we moved to the soda fountain, where he asked George Brolin about Deputy Savage.

"Rick is about as good a guy as they come," the pharmacist said as we sipped our root beer floats. "I had a problem with some kids loitering in front of the pharmacy a few summers ago, and Rick very nicely got them to move on down the road without causing any sort of trouble."

"I guess the soda fountain tends to attract a younger crowd," I observed.

"At times. But I do my best to manage everyone. I don't want my pharmacy customers to feel too intimidated to come inside. A lot of my regulars are seniors who don't necessarily feel comfortable with the vibe teens these days are sending out. And the music they like to blare; don't even get me started."

"Have you considered shutting down the soda fountain?" I

asked as I stirred ice cream into my root beer. Somehow a soda fountain, barbershop, and pharmacy didn't seem a likely combination when it came to customer base.

"Considered it. Been here for over sixty years though. Wouldn't seem right somehow. If I have any trouble, I just mention it to Rick and he takes care of it. His papa started bringing him in here for a cut and a cone when he was just a youngin. Guess he must have been three or four."

"Is Deputy Savage's father still in town?"

"Lives out at the senior home. Rick tried to take care of him on his own, but his dementia got to the point where he really needed round-the-clock care. Rick felt real bad about moving him in to the home at first, but Colin takes good care of Tom, and Rick volunteers at the home as often as he can, so I think it all worked out for the best."

I remembered Colin Walton was the man who'd been given the authority to decide Buck Barnes would be cremated. I didn't know whether the fact that the men obviously knew each other well would play into our investigation, but I made a mental note of the relationship just in case.

"Seems like Deputy Savage spends a lot of time volunteering. Someone mentioned he coaches both adult and kids' sports."

"Rick is an important member of the community. He pitches in more than most. I tell him he should settle down and put some of that energy into a family of his own."

A phone rang in the background. "I best get that. You folks enjoy the rest of your drinks."

"What do you think?" I asked Grandpa.

"I think the more I find out about Deputy Savage the less sure I am that he's intentionally covering up a murder."

"Doc seemed pretty certain the wound to the head couldn't have been caused by a fall."

"Yeah, and Doc knows his stuff."

"Maybe Kyle and Doc will learn something different from what we have so far. Let's go by to have a chat with Mayor Bell. And we should check out the senior home. If the man who runs it is the one who gave the go-ahead to have Buck cremated, I'd like to get a general impression of him."

"Seems like you're spreading yourself a little thin. Are you sure you want to take on this Norton fellow, try to find out whether Savage might be lying about what happened at the house, and figure out whether Buck was really murdered too?"

"I realize I'm taking on a lot, but at this point everything seems equally important. It won't take all that long to speak to the mayor and then we can head to the senior home to try to find out why Mr. Walton had Buck cremated before anyone had a chance to really investigate his death."

"Are we just going to show up and ask to speak to him about the cremation?"

"No, I guess not. I'll call and make an appointment. I'll tell them I have an elderly grandfather who might be interested in their program."

"I'm not that old, and I don't need to be in a home."

"I know that. I'll just make up a story about my maternal grandfather, and once I have his attention, I'll try to work the Buck thing into the conversation."

"This should be interesting," Grandpa Ben said under his breath.

After we left the pharmacy, Grandpa seemed to be in deep thought as he slid into the passenger seat of the car, and I had enough on my mind that I left him with his thoughts and focused on my own.

I called the senior home to see if we could get an appointment for today. I was informed that tours were on Friday mornings and if I wanted to take a look around that would be the time to do so. Grandpa and I discussed our options and decided that the most important thing at this point would be to stop by and have a chat with the mayor about Greg Norton's plans for the island.

I started the car and pulled into traffic. I was beginning to figure out the layout of the town, so finding the mayor's salon didn't present a problem. We headed north and then turned onto Cove Street and parked in the community parking lot. Grandpa decided to wait for me in the car, so I rolled down the windows and hurried across the street. Betty Boop's, much like the name, was an interesting place. For one thing, all three of the hairdressers on duty looked like they had been frozen in time. They all had big hair and colorful makeup that made me wonder if they were on their way to a sock hop.

"Can I help you, darlin'?" the tallest of the three women asked.

"I'm looking for Mayor Bell."

"You found her. What can I do for you? A cut and a blow out?"

I looked around the brightly decorated room. In addition to the three hairdressers there were two women getting their hair done and two others reading magazines.

"No. I'm actually hoping to speak to you in your capacity as mayor. Maybe you can tell me a more convenient time to stop by."

"This is as good a time as any. It looks like our humidity is doing a number on your curls. I can straighten that out for you while we chat."

I touched my hand to my head. I did have a bit of a cavewoman thing going on, but it still wasn't as bad as the 'dos the women who worked in the salon were sporting. "Maybe another time. My grandfather is waiting for me in the car."

"Lordy be, you left the poor man in the car?"

"The windows are down and I only plan to take a minute of your time. I'd prefer to speak to you in private. Perhaps I can make an appointment?"

"Come on back in the morning at around nine. Salon doesn't open until ten, so we can chat while I fix you up real nice."

Terrific. At least the woman had agreed to speak to me in private, and I guessed I could use a trim and maybe a blowout too. My naturally curly hair seemed to have a mind of its own once we hit the humidity of the East Coast. I thanked the woman, assured her I'd see her in the morning, and then headed back to the car.

"So?" Grandpa Ben asked.

"She was busy. I have an appointment to talk with her in the morning. Do you mind making one more stop? I thought I'd run by the inn to see if I can catch Mr. Norton. I'd like to speak to him about his plans before the meeting tomorrow."

"Actually, if you don't mind dropping me at the house I'd like to take a nap before we go out tonight."

"I'd be happy to. The last thing I want is for you to overdo it."

Grandpa Ben required a lot more rest since he'd had a stroke several years ago, so I was happy to have him rest up. After I dropped him off I headed toward the inn. There was no one at the counter when I entered the lobby, so I rang the bell. Hallie smiled as she came into the room.

"Are you still trying to track down Greg Norton?"

"I am. Is he here?"

"Actually, he is. I'll ring up to his room to see if he's willing to speak to you."

"Thanks. I'd appreciate that."

As it turned out, he was happy to speak to me and agreed to meet me in the dining area where the guests took their meals.

"Greg Norton." The man stuck out his hand as soon as he walked up to me.

"Tj Jensen." I shook his hand.

"Let's sit here at a table, shall we?"

I took a seat across from the man, who I could see right off was relaxed and confident, as if he'd already won whatever battle he was geared up to fight.

"What can I do for you, Ms. Jensen?"

"It's come to my attention that you're trying to gain support to force Garrett Hanford to sell his resort to you. I'm here to tell you that Garrett is quite determined not to sell to a developer."

"Yes, I'm aware of Mr. Hanford's very selfish stance."

"Selfish?"

"A megaresort, such as the one the company I work for plans to build, would bring jobs and money to this community. Most of the residents who live on the island barely get by from month to month. By refusing to sell his land to a company with the means to improve it, Mr. Hanford is denying the men and women he claims are his friends the boost in income that very well could make all the difference in their lives."

"Not everyone supports the project," I pointed out.

"That's true, but I think you'll find once I present my final list of supporters at the meeting that a vast majority of the business owners on the island do support the sale of Mr. Hanford's land to Destination Properties."

"What about the turtles that nest on the beach? If you build a big resort, you'll disturb their nesting place."

The man shrugged.

"The turtles can find another beach to nest on. In fact, I have it on good authority that the numbers of nests on the island are diminishing greatly as the turtles move to undeveloped islands in the chain. It really makes no sense that they come to Gull Island in the first place. "

"I heard that you are responsible for the reduction in eggs this year," I challenged.

"A rumor started by small-minded people that cannot be proven. Look, it sounds like you're a friend of Garrett Hanford's and I assume you have his best interests at heart. If you really care about him, you'll convince him to sell the land before things get ugly. I'd hate to see him on the losing side of a battle with his neighbors."

Poor Garrett. He really was in a tough situation. No matter what he did, in the end there were going to be people who wouldn't agree with his decision.

"I can see we're at an impasse. Thank you for your time and I'll see you at the town meeting tomorrow night," I said.

"I'll be looking for you. Talk to Mr. Hanford before it's too late. I can promise him a good price for the land. If he waits until a sale is forced, I guarantee he'll receive substantially less."

Talk about being wound up. I wasn't a huge drinker, especially in the middle of the day, but after my conversation with Norton I found myself heading toward Sully's.

"You're back," Frank greeted me from behind the bar.

"I just finished meeting with your pal Greg Norton and find myself in need of a libation."

Frank laughed. "He does tend to have that effect on people. I have a local brew on tap."

"Sounds perfect." I placed my elbows on the bar and placed my hands on either side of my head in an attempt to ward off the migraine that I knew was just beyond the horizon.

Frank slid a tall frosty glass in front of me. "So tell Frank what the mean man said to make you so upset."

"Why should I tell you anything?"

"I'm the bartender. It's what people do."

I just frowned at the man across the counter from me.

"Really. It's in the bartender handbook. Lesson number

three, after carry a rag over your shoulder and be ready with a lighter, is lend a sympathetic ear."

"You're insane."

"There are those that say that is my most endearing quality. So what did Norton do to bring that scowl to your face?"

"The man is impossible. He doesn't seem to care about the fact that he is basically destroying the island and that the turtle population will suffer greatly. All he cares about is his precious resort. Talking to the man is like talking to a wall."

"Norton may be lacking in social skills, but he knows what he's doing. I know that you'd like to see Garrett's land preserved, but in the end I think you're going to find that you have been knocking your head against the wall for nothing. The guy hasn't spent months on the island just to give up."

I closed my eyes and put my head on the counter. I couldn't remember the last time I'd been this frustrated.

"How about we talk about something else," Frank suggested. "Something less stressful."

"Like what?"

"I hear you've been going around town snooping into Buck's death in spite of the fact that the deputy has declared the man's death due to natural causes."

"You think that's less stressful?"

"Isn't it?"

"Actually, it is. But I'm not snooping. I'm just curious about the man whose body I found in the attic. It's natural to wonder what might have occurred."

"I agree. I liked Buck. He was a good guy who never hurt anyone and didn't deserve to die."

"Finally something we can agree on. I don't suppose that you have any theories you care to share?"

"I know that Buck was hanging around with a couple of men who went by the name Dilly and Lambert before he died."

"Already talked to them. They have alibis."

"You have been busy. I have to give you credit. I figured you were out of your league with this one, but it seems you are on top of things."

"Maybe, but I'm no closer to finding the killer than I was on day one. Actually, that's not true. I have eliminated some of the suspects, so I guess in a way I'm closer to finding the killer. I'm on my way to talk to Digger next."

"Digger?"

"I guess he witnessed some things that others feel might be of interest to me."

"Digger's a tough one to talk to. He tends to be somewhat monosyllabic."

"Thanks for the heads up." I tossed some money on the bar. "And thanks for the talk. I really do feel better."

After I left the bar, I headed to the cemetery where I hoped to find Digger, who should have returned to work today. I really wasn't sure if he could tell me anything that I didn't know, but I supposed it didn't hurt to ask.

Luckily for me, when I arrived at the cemetery Digger was riding a lawn mower and listening to something through headphones. I parked in a designated spot, then wandered across the freshly mowed lawn, looking for a place to position myself so he would see me.

I paused to glance at the headstones I passed as I wandered to the far side of the lawn where Digger was working. It was interesting to find some dating back to the early 1800s mixed in with others that had been set within the past decade. I wasn't sure exactly how that had occurred, but I was certain there was some reason for the placement.

I waved to Digger while he was still a considerable distance away. I hoped that if I gave him enough time to note my presence I wouldn't startle and therefore anger him. I couldn't help but play through my mind the comments made by the others I'd spoken to that week as to the man's instability.

After a moment, he turned off his mower and climbed off. I began to walk closer as he moved toward me. I plastered the largest smile I could muster on my face as I prepared to greet him. "What a lovely spot," I commented. "So serene and peaceful. And the grounds...well, they're about as close to perfection as one can get."

"Can I help you?"

"I was wondering if there've been any burial plans made for Buck Barnes."

"Cremated."

"Yes, I heard. Do you know if there will be a service?"

"Nope."

"I see. It's such a shame what happened to him. I'm sorry, I didn't catch your name."

"Digger."

"I've heard about you. I'm Tj. A few people I've spoken to have sung your praises for all you do for the turtles. I find the turtle rescue team that works on the island fascinating. I understand that an important part of your work consists of protecting the eggs."

Digger smiled and seemed to relax just a bit. "Yes, ma'am."

"I understand that we have several key nests on the beach to the south of the cabins that you make a point to check on."

"Every evening."

"I've been busy in the evenings," I admitted. "Hopefully things will slow down a bit and I can join your group. Was Buck a member of the squad?"

"No. Buck was only interested in one thing and that was treasure."

"I understand you had to keep an eye on him so he didn't disturb the eggs."

"Yup."

"Then maybe you can help me figure out who might have been with Buck on the night he broke into Garrett's place."

"I best get back to work." With that, he climbed onto his mower and drove away.

CHAPTER 11

Grandpa was still napping when I returned home, and no one else seemed to be around, so I decided to take a look in the attic. It occurred to me that Deputy Savage came back on the day after we'd found Buck's remains for a reason. He'd said he wanted to look around, but my gut told me he was interested in something specific. If Buck found something that got him killed, maybe I could figure out what it was.

Attics could be so interesting to explore. There was something about them that whispered secrets long buried by the generations of men, women, and children who'd stored their most precious memories and prized possessions within those very walls. Garrett's attic was filled with the items you'd expect to find: boxes, old furniture, and discarded household items, including a dressmaker's mannequin and a rusted bicycle.

I knelt down to right a stack of photos that had been carelessly spilled from a box onto the hardwood floor. One photo in particular caught my eye. It didn't look as old as some of the others and showed a young man holding a toddler. He stood in front of this house next to a young woman with a strong chin and a look of determination in her eye. I couldn't know for certain, but if I had to guess, this was Garrett as a young child with his mother and father.

I returned all the photos to the box, then stood up and looked around. It seemed that there was an angle we might be missing. If Buck was indeed in the attic to look for the map, it made sense he would have thoroughly searched the boxes stacked around the room. What if in the course of searching for the map he found something else?

I heard a slight rustling sound that I couldn't quite identify. I looked at the window Blackbeard had flown in through the day we arrived, but it was closed now, as it had been since then. I looked back toward the spot where we'd discovered Buck Barnes's remains and my mind shifted from hidden treasure to ghostly spirits with unresolved issues. I was about to turn off the light and go back downstairs when I heard the rustling sound again. This time I could tell it was coming from the far corner of the attic.

"Buck?" I whispered.

My inquiry was met with silence.

I was just being silly. I didn't believe in ghosts. It was just the eeriness of the room, covered in dust and cobwebs, that had taken hold of my imagination. I turned again to turn off the light just as a box that had been stacked atop others fell to the floor, creating not only a loud crash but a cloud of dust.

I jumped as my heart skipped a beat. "Buck? Is that you?"

There was no answer, and I slowly took a step toward the corner of the attic. The scurrying sound had returned, which, given my heightened state of awareness, suggested something from the opening scene of every slasher movie I'd ever seen. I knew it would make more sense to turn around and head for the safety of the floors below, but my mind refused to let go of what might be found beyond the stack of boxes.

I held my breath as I slowly walked to what turned out to be a pile of old home movies. I could feel my heart pounding in my chest as I caught a flash of movement created by a shadow. I wasn't sure exactly what I expected to find, but I felt nothing but relief when my ghost turned out to have a shaggy orange tail.

"Cuervo, what are you doing up here?"

"Meow."

I picked up the large orange cat. I had left the door open and Cuervo was just the sort to view the open passageway as an invitation to investigate.

"You about scared the life out of me. I know you're curious, but I really do think we should head downstairs after we clean up the mess you made."

Cuervo struggled to get down. He wasn't the most affectionate cat in the world, so I set him on the floor before I ended up with scratches on my arms. As soon as his paws hit the floor he trotted over to a wall and pawed at the small opening created by a fault in the paneling.

"Do you hear a mouse?"

"Meow."

"I know you fancy yourself a big brave warrior who has vowed to rid the place of rodents, but I think this one time we can leave the poor thing free to go about his business. Let's go downstairs and I'll find the salmon treats."

Cuervo ignored me, which wasn't at all odd because he tended to ignore me unless it served his purposes to do otherwise. I didn't want to risk being mauled by his sharp claws, but I didn't want to leave him alone in the attic either, so I bent down to try to talk some sense into him.

"If there even is a mouse in the wall there's no way to get it. Let's head down for a snack."

Cuervo continued to paw at the wall.

"There's nothing there. See." I tried to show him that the flaw in the wood was just that, a flaw. I ran my hand over the wall and was about to attempt to pick the cat up once more when I noticed that a corner of the panel had been pulled away.

The dust near the panel was marred in such a way as to suggest that someone had recently tampered with it. I stuck my hand into the panel and gave it a gentle tug. Behind the panel I found a document, which I pulled out and unrolled. "Well, I'll be. Cuervo, it looks like you just found the map to Barkley's treasure."

I picked up Cuervo and headed back downstairs. Kyle had come in from his walk so I showed him the map.

"It does look like a treasure map," Kylie confirmed. "But it doesn't look old enough to have belonged to the pirate known as John Barkley. According to Meg, Barkley had lived on the island in the late 1600s. I won't claim to be an expert on antiquities, but based on the material used, this map looks as if it can't be older than one, maybe two hundred years at the most."

"How can we find out for sure?"

"I have a friend who works for a museum. I guess I can call him and ask if he'll take a look at it. In the meantime, I guess we can call Garrett and ask him if he knows anything about the map."

"I'll call him," I offered. "I've been meaning to check in with him anyway."

"Were you planning to tell him about the town meeting?"

"Not yet. I want to speak to the mayor first so that I have all the facts before I burden him with the chaos that's been going on in his absence."

"Yeah, I guess that's a good idea. Ask him if he knows what 'Charlie bad' means. Blackbeard has been repeating those words over and over again. I almost feel like he's trying to tell me something."

"Yeah, I've heard him say the same thing. Maybe he picked it up from a movie."

Kyle shrugged. "Could be, but it couldn't hurt to ask."

I took my cell phone out onto the deck and made my call.

Luckily, Garrett picked up by the third ring.

"Garrett, it's Tj."

"Good morning, darlin'. So nice of you to check in on me."

"How are you feeling today?"

"Not bad. Not bad at all. I have my good days and my bad ones, and it looks like this one is going to be a good one."

"I'm so glad."

"How's Blackbeard doing?"

"He's doing just great. Kyle has taken a real liking to the bird. Gracie too. The three of them have been playing pirate."

Garrett chuckled. "Blackbeard loves to play pirate. When I first got him he didn't talk as much as he does now, but the few things he did say had to do with pirates and pirate ships. I have a feeling his previous owner purchased him for the purpose of acting out his pirate fantasies."

"So you aren't Blackbeard's original owner?"

"No. He was still a young bird when I found him, but I wasn't his first owner."

I curled my legs up under my body and adjusted my position on the lounger as I settled in for a long conversation. "You found him? I just assumed you purchased him."

"Nope. I was out in the yard one day and the bird flew up and landed on my shoulder. Talk about startled. Luckily, I had the presence of mind not to totally freak out and scare the poor guy. I said something to him—I honestly can't remember what—and he responded with 'find the treasure.' I took him inside and called the local veterinarian. I asked if anyone was missing a parrot, but no one was. I ran an ad in the paper, but no one ever claimed him, so I kept him. We've been together ever since. He's been the perfect companion. He talks but not incessantly, and he loves to watch old movies as much as I do. He's the one who turned me on to pirate movies, but now we both love them."

I smiled.

"What a great story. We've had a lot of fun with him. He seems to actually be communicating and not just parroting words back to us."

"Oh, Blackbeard can communicate. Don't doubt that for a minute. He uses words he knows, but the meaning is clear. When he's hungry he'll say 'feed the bird,' and when he gets mad at me he tells me to 'walk the plank.' He's very intelligent."

"Any idea what 'Charlie bad' might mean?"

Garrett didn't answer right away. Then he said, "I don't have a clue. We like to watch Charlie Chaplin movies, but I've never heard him refer to Charlie as bad. I've heard him mention 'Charlie's hat.' He seems fascinated with that hat. We watched *Charlie's Angels*, but Blackbeard usually would just say 'pretty girl' or 'what a babe.' I can assure you he learned that from his previous owner as well."

"Have you ever heard him use the word 'bad' in any other context?"

"Yeah. He seems to understand the concept of bad, which is amazing if you think about it. To be honest, I tend to take the fact that Blackbeard can communicate so well for granted."

Garrett and I talked about Blackbeard for a while longer before I changed the subject to the map I'd found in the wall of his attic. "I have some news you may find surprising."

"Could use a surprise."

"I was in the attic a while ago, trying to straighten up a bit, and I found an old map hidden in the wall."

"A map? What map?"

That seemed to answer the question as to whether Garrett knew about it and could even have put it there himself. "I'm not really sure. I thought you might know."

"Don't know nothin' about any map. My mother told me she destroyed the one to Barkley's treasure that my dad had, and that's the only map I ever heard anyone talk about."

I tucked my feet up under my legs to make room for Echo, who'd chosen that moment to sit directly in front of me. "We don't know what this map leads to, but we're certain it isn't old enough to have belonged to a pirate who lived in the seventeenth century."

"You think there's *another* treasure hidden on Gull Island?"

"I don't know." Echo put his paw on my lap and I gave him a scratch on the head. "What I do know is that it looked as if someone has accessed the map's hiding place recently. It really doesn't make sense that someone would find it and then leave it behind, but the paneling had been partially pulled away from the wall and there were fingerprints in the dust on the wall where the paneling had been tampered with. I have no way of knowing if it was involved in Buck Barnes's murder, but it seems possible, even likely."

"Murder?" Garrett sounded surprised. "I spoke to Savage and he said that after he looked into it, he determined Buck died of natural causes."

"Yeah, that's the story he's telling everyone, but I don't buy it."

"Rick wouldn't lie." Garrett seemed adamant. "He's a good guy. Besides, what reason could he possibly have for doing so?"

"I'm not sure," I admitted. "Right now we're operating under the assumption that someone killed Buck, Savage knows who it was, and he's protecting that person."

"That don't make a lick of sense. Rick wouldn't lie to protect a killer. Besides, he liked Buck. If he was murdered, Rick would want to find the killer as much as anyone. I know you mean well, Tj, but you have to trust me on this: Rick wouldn't cover up a crime, particularly a murder."

I didn't doubt Garrett believed what he was saying, but I was still sure that for whatever reason, Deputy Savage was doing just that.

We spoke for a few more minutes and then I signed off after promising to call him again the following day.

"So?" Kyle asked, joining me on the porch.

"He didn't know anything about the map."

"I've given it a lot of thought, and even though it can't be the map to a treasure left on the island by John Barkley, it could be the map Garrett's great-grandfather found in the vault. I wonder if he just assumed the map was to Barkley's treasure when it actually led to something else entirely."

"Maybe. One thing's for sure: if this *is* the map Garrett's great-grandfather found, it's been responsible for a lot of heartache."

Kyle sat down next to me, a puzzled look on his face. "The thing I don't get is how whoever found the map knew it was there. Garrett told you he didn't know of its existence, and his dad has been dead for a long time. I suppose Garrett's mother might just have hidden the map rather than destroying it, but why tell anyone if she didn't want it found?"

"All very good questions I'm afraid we may never have answers to."

CHAPTER 12

By the time Ben woke up from his nap and Doc returned from his day in town, it was time to pick up the girls from the kids' camp and begin assembling the things we'd need for our first-ever movie on the beach. I had to admit that I was as excited as the girls.

"Can we bring our swimsuits?" Gracie asked as she watched me dig through the closet for a blanket to sit on.

"No, sweetie. We won't be swimming tonight."

"But it's hot."

"It won't be once the sun goes down. I do want you to grab some sunscreen though. As a precaution."

"Can Pumpkin come?"

"I don't think dogs are allowed. Be sure to grab a sweatshirt. And tell Ashley to grab one as well."

"Ashley won't let me go into her room."

I stopped what I was doing and looked directly at Gracie. "Why not?"

"Because she's on the phone with her boyfriend and she said she needs her privacy."

"Her boyfriend?" Ashley was only eleven.

"She met him today at kids' camp. His name is Gordon and he's a nerd."

I found the blanket I was looking for and closed the closet door. "Nerd in a good way, as in he's really smart, or nerd in a bad way, as in he's annoying?"

"The second one. Can we bring popcorn?"

"I think they're supposed to be selling food. At least I hope they are, because I'm not bringing any. Now I need you to run upstairs and grab a sweatshirt and sunscreen. Knock on Ashley's door nicely and tell her to grab a sweatshirt too."

"But..."

"Please, Gracie? Grandpa, Kyle, and Doc are waiting for us, and I still need to make sure the dogs have food and water."

"Okay," Gracie grumbled as she headed for the stairs.

I wondered if Ashley actually had a boyfriend or if Gracie was just making that up. I wanted to think she was much too young for such things, but I remembered I'd had a boyfriend when I was her age. It wasn't serious, of course, and the romance part of it had amounted to a few stolen kisses behind the school building during recess.

Still, I remembered feeling vulnerable and a little scared about how to handle the sensations I was feeling. Maybe I needed to have a talk with Ash sooner rather than later. For now, though, I needed to get myself and the girls out the door before one of the seniors with whom I shared my life started hollering for us to get a move on.

The drive to the beach was a short one. When we arrived at the stretch of sand designated for the movie, we were greeted by an array of colorful blankets that seemed to cover almost every square inch of ground for as far as the eye could see.

"I guess we should have come earlier," I stated the obvious.

"When Gertie said this was a popular event I had no idea this is what she meant," Doc agreed.

"Look, there's Gertie over there." Ashley pointed in her direction. "She's waving us over."

I grabbed Gracie's hand as we made our way through the sea of bodies. I was afraid if I lost her in the crowd I'd never find her again. I found myself swept up in the festive energy as people gathered together to catch up and discuss local gossip.

"So glad you made it." Gertie gave Doc a peck on the cheek. "I saved a large enough space for all of us if we snuggle up real close."

"Thank you," I said as I dropped my own blanket atop hers. "I had no idea there would be this big a crowd. I guess we should have come earlier." I looked around. "A lot earlier."

"A lot of folks come in the morning and spend the day. Attendance drops off a bit once we get into the heat of July and August, but it's still a good idea to at least bring a blanket by and stake out your spot."

"If you bring a blanket in the morning is it still here by evening?" Doc asked.

"Most times. I've been doing that for years and I've only lost two blankets so far. It's a risk, but as long as you have a blanket you're willing to lose it's worth the effort." Gertie turned toward Ashley and Gracie. "Are you girls hungry? There are several food trucks in the parking lot."

Ashley and Gracie were hungry, so we went to get food while Doc waited with Gertie. The food trucks were arranged in a straight line. There were five trucks in all, each featuring a different type of food. One truck served tacos, burritos, and other Mexican fare, while another served burgers, hotdogs, and fries. Kyle focused on a truck that served gyros, while my grandfather chose fish and chips and the girls opted for burgers and fries. I was about to settle for a turkey sub when I noticed the truck with freshly grilled kabobs made from an assortment of vegetables and either pork, beef, chicken, or shrimp.

"Look, there's Willow." Ashley waved as I got into line at the kabob truck. "Can I go say hi?"

"Me too?" Gracie enthusiastically chimed in.

"Sure, as long as you stay together. Say hi and come right back. I don't want to lose you in the crowd."

I watched as the girls ran over to greet Willow, who was headed toward Kyle, who was waiting with Ben. She had a curly-haired toddler with her who looked to be one, maybe two at the most. The child reached for Kyle as soon as he was within reach. Kyle opened his arms to the toddler, who squealed with delight when Kyle hoisted her onto his shoulders. Ashley said something to Willow, who looked toward where I was standing and waved.

"Can I help you?"

"I need two kabobs. One shrimp and one chicken."

"Jerk?"

"Come again?" I asked.

"What type of grilling sauce would you prefer? Jerk is popular with the shrimp."

"Oh, okay, jerk is fine."

By the time I'd paid for and received my food, Ben and the girls were heading in my direction. One bite of the spicy shrimp and I realized I should have ordered something to drink.

"Uncle Kyle said to head on back with the food. He'll meet us in a few minutes," Ashley informed me.

"Is that Willow's daughter?"

"Yeah, isn't she cute? Her name is Hannah."

"She sure seems to like Kyle."

"All the kids love Kyle," Ashley said. "When he was at the camp the other day he had half the kids there following him around. Willow is talking to him about volunteering on Friday. We're going to have a beach and barbeque day."

"Sounds like fun."

"You should come," Gracie encouraged.

"I'd love to, but Grandpa and I have an appointment in town on Friday."

"That's fine." Gracie sighed.

I felt bad that I had to miss the outing, but I really did want to check out the Gull Island Senior Home. I'd have to make more of an effort to help out at the kids' camp once things settled down a bit.

After we returned to the blanket, Doc and Gertie went for food. The movie wouldn't actually begin until it was completely dark, which at this time of year was at around nine, though the crowd that had gathered didn't seem to mind in the least as they made the best of the warm summer evening. Tonight we were going to see a movie from the eighties, *One Crazy Summer*. I'd discovered the movie committee liked to mix things up and show movies from all eras. The previous movie had been a recent production that had been in the movie theaters less than a year earlier, while later in the summer there were plans to show some silent movies from the twenties.

I wasn't sure how much the girls would enjoy the antics of screen actors like Charlie Chaplin and Jean Harlow, but I did hope Garrett was back by then because Gertie had mentioned that the idea for the old black and whites had been his in the first place.

"Is Meg planning to see the movie this evening?" I asked Ben.

"She said she was going to try to make it. Her daughter is in town and the two of them were having dinner, but she was going to come by after if the opportunity presented itself."

"So her daughter doesn't live on the island?"

"She lives in Chicago. She's an attorney. Seems she's on her way to a conference in Atlanta but took a couple of extra days to come by to visit her mother. I mentioned the map you found this afternoon to her and she said she'd very much like to take a look at it."

"Did you tell her that, although we're pretty sure the map couldn't have belonged to John Barkley, we wanted to keep the fact that we have a map under wraps for a while?"

"I did. You can trust Meg. She won't tell anyone about it. She's really just interested in it for the historical significance. Oh, look, there she is now."

I greeted Meg and asked her about her daughter. We chatted about local news while we finished our meal. Kyle still hadn't rejoined us by the time we'd finished eating and Doc and Gertie had returned with their own meals, so I left the girls with the seniors and went to look for him. I realized he was a grown man and most likely hadn't gotten lost in the crowd, but I wondered if there really could be something between him and Willow. She seemed like a lovely person, but I couldn't help but feel a tiny bit jealous. Kyle and I weren't a couple, but I acknowledged that my feelings for him had become increasingly complicated lately.

I thought part of my confusion stemmed from the fact that I had grown to depend on him so much. He'd been my rock through all the changes I'd been through, and while I didn't know whether the two of us were meant to ever become something more than close friends, I wasn't ready for him to become a couple with anyone else. I realized that was irrational and completely unfair, but sometimes feelings were simply what they were—feelings—whether they were rational or not.

I touched my lips as I thought about our almost kiss. Again. I'd spent more time than I should replaying the moment in my mind, trying to figure out if I had imagined the tilt of his head toward mine. Somewhere along the way I'd pretty much decided the almost kiss was really nothing more than a figment of my imagination.

One thing was certain: Kyle seemed exactly like himself since that moment. Any weirdness I would have expected to result from such an intimate moment simply didn't exist, so maybe, like the weirdness, the intimacy I'd imagined really didn't exist.

I stopped and looked around at the throngs of people who seemed to be traveling in every direction. I might as well head back to the others. I was never going to find Kyle in all of this. I was about to turn around when I noticed Toby in the distance. I decided to go and have a chat with him on the off chance that he was in a more talkative mood than he'd been in when I spoke to him the other day.

"You still trying to track down Buck's killer?" Toby asked after I greeted him.

"I am. Do you have anything to add?"

"Gave it some more thought after you left and I may have a couple more names for you." He spat the tobacco he was chewing onto the ground.

I cringed. Talk about gross. "Okay, great. Who?"

"Greg Norton."

Norton was already on my suspect list, but I was interested to hear his reasoning, so I asked him why he thought he would want to kill Buck.

"I don't rightly know that, but I did see them talking a time or two before Buck died, and I happen to know they were together out at Garrett's place at least a couple of times."

"You saw them together?" I clarified.

"No. I didn't actually see them, but people talk and I listen."

"Who did you hear about Norton from?"

"Mamie Sue. She works with the turtle lady."

So far Toby was just telling me things that I already knew.

"Okay. Who else do you have?"

"There's a guy named Digger who has been feuding with

Buck for years over those turtle nests. Guess Buck disturbed the eggs a time or two while he was searching on the beach for whatever treasure he was after, which didn't sit well with Digger."

"And you think Digger would kill Buck over something like that?"

"The guy is a nutcase. He once chased me with an ax for digging on the beach and I was nowhere near a nest. He made a comment about holes on the beach creating obstacles for the baby turtles once they hatched and began their long dangerous journey to the sea."

"I suppose he had a point."

"He chased me with an ax," Toby emphasized.

"I guess that *is* a bit much," I admitted. I supposed if Digger caught Buck searching near the nests he might have followed him back to the house and hit him with something. I didn't get the sense that Digger was guilty of anything when I'd spoken to him, but I supposed it wouldn't hurt to have another conversation with the man. "You've been very helpful. Do you have anyone else to add to the list?"

Toby pointed. "See that guy in the orange shirt?"

"Yeah."

"His name is Gil. He's a treasure hunter like me. I heard the two partnered on a project recently. I don't know for a fact that he killed Buck, but I do know the two had a falling out of sorts."

"Do you know what the falling out was about?"

"Actually, I don't. Just passing along what I heard."

"Okay, thanks. I'll go and have a chat with him now. Thanks again."

I kept my eye on the orange shirt as I headed through the crowd. Luckily, Gil was standing still, talking to someone and not moving around, because I would have lost him for sure in the crowd.

"Gil," I greeted the man, who looked and smelled like he hadn't bathed in a month.

"Yeah?"

"My name is Tj. I was hoping to speak with you about Buck Barnes."

"What about him?"

"I understand the two of you partnered on a project recently."

"Guess you heard wrong. After what Buck did to me the last time we came to an agreement, I'd have to be a fool to pair up with him again."

"The last time?"

"Fool told me he had a map that was going to lead him to a treasure worth a fortune. I spend two months digging up the island only to find the map Buck said he had was just a drawing of a map he'd copied from a book. Guess I should have insisted on seeing the map sooner, but Buck was being real secretive about things and I was new to the island, so I figured what the heck. What a waste of time that was."

"And you hadn't worked with Buck since?" I verified.

"No, I hadn't."

"Do you know who he might have been partnered with recently?'

"No one local, I can tell you that. The guy had earned himself a reputation for taking his partners on nothing but wild goose chases."

Several people had made similar comments, yet it did seem that Buck had been pretty successful in pulling others into his fantasies. "I guess you heard Adam Joyner worked with him for a while."

"You talking about the guy who works at the post office?"

"Yeah."

"I don't have any details, but I think that was a very

temporary thing. Look, I really don't know nothin', though it does seem I've helped you out here, wouldn't you say?"

I frowned. "I guess so."

"Don't you think that would be worth something?"

"You want money?"

"I wouldn't turn it down."

I somewhat reluctantly handed the man a twenty, which he accepted with his left hand. I suspected he had lost the use of his right hand, which I noticed hung limply at his side. Based on the injury to Buck's head, Doc was fairly certain that the person who had hit him had been right handed. I mentally crossed Gil off my suspect list and would do so physically after I confirmed my suspicion with Doc. That left me again with Greg Norton, who was still, at that point, my number one suspect, and Digger, who came in at a distant second after my conversation with Toby. I was on my way back to the others when I found Kyle, not with Willow but standing off to the side of the crowd, talking on his phone. When he saw me he waved me over, so I joined him and waited while he completed his call.

"That was my friend from the museum," Kyle informed me once he'd hung up. "Based on the photo I sent him, he agrees the map you found in the attic most likely isn't more than a hundred years old, two at the most. He offered to take a closer look at it if I overnighted it to him, so I'm going to do that tomorrow."

"Okay, so what are we thinking? That this is a different map from the one Garrett's grandfather claimed to have found, or that he'd found the map we discovered in the attic and jumped to the conclusion that it was the one referred to in the legend?"

"I don't know. I don't see how we can know."

I paused as I considered what, if anything, my discovery of the map meant. Kyle was right; there was no way for us to know if the map I'd found in the wall was the same one Garrett's father and grandfather believed once belonged to Captain John Barkley, but we did know someone had recently accessed the hiding place. Could it have been Buck Barnes?

"Do you think the map and the killer are related even if the map doesn't lead to Barkley's treasure?" Kyle asked.

"I don't know. My number one suspect is still Greg Norton. I really want him to be the killer, but if you look at things objectively, that doesn't make sense."

"Why do you say that?" Kyle asked.

"For one thing, if Deputy Savage really is covering up the murder there's no way he'd do it to protect Norton."

"Unless he's being bribed."

I remembered the tender way the deputy had looked at the kittens. Maybe I was letting sentiment get in the way, but I just couldn't believe a man of such compassion was covering up a murder in order to make a buck.

"No, I don't think that's it. If he *is* covering up the murder, he must be doing it to protect someone. I don't have all this straight in my mind, but it looks like the movie is about to start. Should we head back?"

"Yeah, just let me just say goodbye to Willow and Riley. I was talking to them when I got the phone call." Kyle took my hand and led me through the crowd.

"Riley?"

"Willow's boyfriend. I just met him tonight, but he seems like a nice guy. I'm sure you'll like him. I thought the four of us might go sailing one day soon. They rent boats in the marina, and I've wanted to go out ever since we've been here. I mentioned it to Riley and he said his father used to own a boat and they went out frequently until he passed away a few years ago."

"That sounds like fun. I imagine sailing in the ocean is quite a bit different from sailing on the lake."

"It can be. The experience is similar, as long as you go on a day when the water isn't too rough."

Kyle was right; I liked Riley the moment I met him. He was friendly and funny and seemed to be totally taken with both Willow and her daughter. I had a feeling that now that my ridiculous feelings of jealousy were out of the way, the four of us were going to be great friends. He even talked me into volunteering for the annual Fourth of July celebration that was held on the island every year. The event was similar to the ones held all over the country. There was a pancake breakfast, a parade, a community picnic, a kiddie carnival, and fireworks in the evening. What made the celebration on Gull Island unique was the mock treasure hunt, when teams signed up to follow a map to a treasure that was planted by the island council.

"It's pretty awesome," Riley continued. "The treasure is planted, but the thrill of the hunt is real."

"It sounds like a lot of fun." I looked at Kyle. "Want to team up and try it?"

"Sure."

"The committee goes to a lot of effort to make it seem real. They even age the maps to make them look like they could be hundreds of years old. There's a different treasure and a different map every year, so the hunt is never the same."

It was well past everyone's bedtime by the time we got home. Kyle carried Ashley up to her room while I followed with Gracie. I tucked both girls in while Kyle took the dogs out for a quick walk. Both Grandpa and Doc had turned in while I was seeing to the girls, so I poured myself a glass of wine and went out onto the deck to wait for Kyle.

It was another peaceful evening. The stars looked like diamonds in the moonless sky. The air temperature had cooled from the heat of the day, so I was quite comfortable with a light sweater to ward off the chill.

I relaxed on the lounger and let the sound of the waves lull me into a state of semi-consciousness. It was hard to believe we'd only just arrived on the islands six days earlier. We'd barely finished unpacking when the friendly locals had made us feel like a part of the family.

I opened my eyes when I felt a wet kiss on my cheek. "I love you too, Echo."

Echo wagged his tail while Kyle, Pumpkin, and Trooper made their way toward me.

"I figured you would have headed straight to bed," Kyle commented. "It seemed like you could barely stay awake during the movie."

"I just wanted a few minutes to unwind. How was your walk?"

"Nice. I love how warm the water is. I might try a moonlight swim one of these nights. Tonight, however, I'm going to head in. I'm exhausted."

"Yeah, me too." I yawned as I shifted my body into a more comfortable position. "I've been thinking about the map. Riley mentioned that the town uses a process to make the maps that are handed out for the annual treasure hunt look old. Do you think the map I found could simply be one of the maps from the local event? Riley said the treasure hunt had been held for almost fifty years."

I couldn't see Kyle's face in the darkness, but I could sense a frown as he considered my theory.

"I'm pretty sure the map isn't old enough to have belonged to Barkley, but I do think it's older than fifty years. Still, you have an interesting theory that might be worth looking into. I wonder if anyone keeps copies of the maps that have been used in the past."

"That sounds like a Meg thing. Maps from past treasure hunts sound like something the museum might keep on file."

"Yeah, maybe. I'll take it over to the museum tomorrow before I send it off to my friend. If it's just a prop, finding out sooner rather than later will save everyone some time and energy."

"I'll go with you. We can go after we drop the girls off at camp in the morning."

"Actually, I talked to the girls about sleeping in and heading to camp in the afternoon for the beach day. We can pay Meg a visit when everyone is up. I think the museum opens at ten."

CHAPTER 13

Thursday, June 22

Due to the late night, everyone was still asleep when I left for my appointment with Mayor Bell. I wasn't sure what, if anything, she could tell me, but I figured it was worth the time to check it out. Unfortunately, she insisted on trimming my hair and blow drying it while we chatted. Anyone who knew me was aware that my hair was long and curly and generally unruly, so I tended to just keep it pulled back in a braid or ponytail.

"Just a very light trim," I instructed. "Less than an inch."

"Don't worry, sugar, I'll fix you right up. Why don't you tell me what's on your mind?"

"I wanted to speak to you about the town meeting tonight."

"I pretty much figured that was what you were after. I'm afraid the meeting has all the makings of a potentially vol-a-tile situation."

I found the way she dragged out the word "volatile" to be a bit intimidating. "I'm having a hard time understanding exactly what's going on. Some of the people I've spoken to have made it sound like if Mr. Norton gets enough support, Garrett can be forced to sell to his company whether he wants to or not."

Betty frowned and her entire demeanor changed. It seemed as if Betty the hairdresser was gone and Betty the mayor had taken her place.

"It's not quite as simple as that, although I do think Norton and his supporters are hoping to garner enough backing that the option of using eminent domain to force Garrett to hand over his land is a real option."

I frowned. Betty was all business and very serious. I could see why she'd been elected mayor. "I thought eminent domain was only used for cases associated with public use, like freeways and utilities."

"You ever thought about bangs?"

And just like that Betty the hairdresser was back.

"Absolutely not. Please, just a very light trim. The longer my hair is, the easier it is to handle. So about the eminent domain...?"

Betty paused, the serious expression returning to her face. "There have been a number of cases in recent years when developers were successful in using eminent domain for private enterprise, usually in resort areas. A case must be made that the project will benefit the community as a whole and will bring a new level of prosperity to the area, which is what Norton is trying to prove. It's unfortunate that Garrett isn't here on the island. I think Norton would have had a lot less success if those signing his petition had to look Garrett in the eye."

"Do you think Norton will be successful?"

"Honestly, without Garrett's cooperation Destination Properties has a long road ahead of them. I doubt the company will want to deal with any lawsuit Garrett might initiate, plus there are environmental issues that could come into play. It's my opinion Norton is aware of that and is actually banking on the fact that once Garrett sees how much support he has, he'll give in and sell the property to his employer."

"Do you mind if I ask where you stand on all of this?" I asked.

Betty ran her fingers through my hair, as if trying to make up her mind about something, which I hoped had nothing to do with layers. "Personally, I'm torn. I've lived on this island my entire life. I love it here and wouldn't want to live anywhere else, but I'm also a business owner, so I do understand how difficult it is to make a living here. It's like Betty Sue the lifelong resident wants to see what we have here maintained, while Betty Sue the businesswoman can't help but welcome a chance to have a healthier bottom line, and then there's Betty Sue the mayor, who needs to be neutral so as to take the needs of all those who elected her into account."

"Do you plan to come out for or against the project at the meeting tonight?"

"At this point I don't plan to do either. My role in this whole thing will be to keep neighbors from killing one another once the discussion becomes heated, which, trust me, it's going to."

I sat and thought about things as Betty Sue dried my hair. I supposed the only thing I could do was to talk to Garrett to make certain of exactly where he stood on the issue and then to try to represent his interests to the best of my ability. I had to agree with Betty Sue; there was no way the meeting tonight was going to end without bloodshed, either physical or metaphorical.

"What do you think?" Betty Sue asked after she finished with my hair.

I had to admit I looked really different with neatly trimmed and perfectly straight hair. "I like it. Of course I'm not sure how long the straightness will last."

"I put some product in your hair, so it should hold until you get it wet."

"Thank you. How much do I owe you?"

"It's on the house."

"Thank you; that's very kind. I guess I'll see you at the meeting tonight."

"I guess you will."

I left the beauty salon and decided to head down the street for a cup of coffee. It was early, and chances were the family was still asleep.

Many of the shops had begun to decorate for the upcoming Fourth of July festivities, creating a sea of red, white, and blue for as far as the eye could see. In spite of everything that had occurred in the short time I'd been on the island, I definitely was enjoying the change in scenery and the opportunity to gain a new perspective. Maybe I even walked into the coffee bar with a spring in my step. Unfortunately, Greg Norton was sitting in there enjoying his own hot beverage, which deflated my good mood significantly.

"Are you hoping that if you get all dolled up you'll be able to convince more of the townsfolk to come over to your way of thinking?" he asked.

I ignored the man's question and asked one of my own. "Do you really believe a megaresort is the right thing for this island?"

"I do, and even if I didn't, it's my job to carry out the desires of my employer."

"You know Garrett is never going to agree to sell to you. Why don't you take your blueprints and find another island to destroy?"

"You're a feisty one. I like that in a woman. In fact, I like you, but that doesn't mean I'm going to back down. There are a lot of folks on this island who welcome the opportunity to boost their income. The resort Destination Properties plans to build will bring a lot of capital here. It's my job to make sure that happens, which I intend to do. Now, if you'll excuse me, I have a few more undecideds to convince to see things my way."

Norton pushed back his chair and stood up.

I reached out and grabbed his arm. "Before you go, I have a source who told me you were seen out at Garrett's place with Buck Barnes right before he died. Would you care to tell me what the two of you were doing there?"

Norton frowned. He pulled a perfectly white handkerchief out of his pocket and wiped his hands on it before returning it to his pocket. "Actually, I think in this case I'll decline to reply. I'll see you tonight." He had the nerve to wink at me before he left.

I wasn't certain what was going to happen that night, but one thing was for sure: it wouldn't be boring.

As I returned to the resort I made the decision that I really did need to call Garrett again, even though it wasn't a conversation I wanted to have.

"Didn't expect you to call so early. Is everything all right?" Garrett asked.

"Everything is fine. I just never got around to talking to you about the resort yesterday and wanted to see if you'd spoken to Jack." I knew I should get directly to the point of this call, but now that I had Garrett on the phone I found myself wavering. The poor guy really did have a lot to deal with and I hated to be the bearer of more bad news.

"I did speak to Jack about his idea of subdividing the land," Garrett said. "To be honest, I'm not sure what I think about the whole thing, but I told him I'd be willing to look at his plans. It's going to be hard enough on me to have to sell the resort. Seems like cutting it into small pieces will be even worse."

I crossed the room and sat down on the sofa. "Yeah, I get that. Change in any form is difficult, and the more severe the change the harder it can be. I wish I could make this easier for you. I grew up on a resort, so I understand how you can become invested in every little aspect of the property. You have your favorite spots where you like to take time for yourself, your favorite traditions with the changing of the seasons, as well as your favorite customers who return every year and feel like family. I know it would kill my dad if he were forced to carve up Maggie's Hideaway. The resort is almost like a second child to him."

"Exactly. I knew I chose the right person to oversee this project."

"Having said that," I added, "Jack has a point. It's going to cost a lot of money to renovate the resort as it now stands. Probably more than you would be able to recover. And there's something more that may affect the whole thing that I really wish I didn't have to tell you."

"Something more?"

I explained about the town meeting and the fact that the man who was in town to take from Garrett what he didn't seem to be willing to sell had managed to garner quite a bit of support for his petition.

My words were met with silence. I could hear Garrett breathing, so I knew I hadn't lost the connection.

"I guess what I need from you is some direction," I continued. "I plan to attend the meeting tonight and I'll do my best to ensure that your desires for the resort are known and understood, but I need to know whether you've changed your mind in any way given this situation. If you choose to fight Mr. Norton, my sense is that it won't be pleasant."

"I should be there. I knew Norton was snooping around, but I had no idea he'd made so much progress. I guess I thought that if I ignored him, he'd go away."

"I understand why you might feel you need to be here, but I can assure you that I'll do my best in your absence."

"There's no way I'm letting that man or his company destroy what my family spent generations building and protecting. It's not just about the resort. It's about the land and the turtles and a way of life that isn't at all congruent with a large resort with hundreds of guests. What time is the meeting?"

"It's at seven, but I don't think it would be a good idea for you to try to be here. You've had a major stroke. Your body is still healing. Your health is the most important thing right now."

"Let's be realistic. My health issues are going to prevent me from living a long life. I most likely only have a few years left on this earth. As far as I'm concerned, the most important thing to me to do with my time left is to find a buyer who will love the resort as much as I do. I need to know that the land and wildlife that make their home on the beach and in the marsh will prosper long after I'm gone. There's no way I'm going to sit by and let Destination Properties build their megaresort. I know I should stay here and do my physical therapy, but I need to be there."

I had to admit that when Garrett spoke with conviction about the land he loved his passion brought a chill to my spine. It would benefit Garrett's cause if he could stand in front of his neighbors and look them in the eye, but I hated to see him take a turn physically, which is exactly what I feared would happen if he made the trip. There didn't seem to be a good answer to the dilemma. Unless..."I have an idea how you can do both."

"Was that Garrett?" Kyle asked as I hung up the phone.

"It was."

"How'd it go?"

"As I expected, he was upset. More than upset; he was furious. It took everything I had to keep him from arranging for a ride and heading to the island."

"I can understand that. He must feel completely helpless."

"He does. But I had an idea. Can you help me set up some audio/video equipment over at the town hall?"

"Sure, I guess. Why?"

"I'm going to dial Garrett into the meeting so he can stay at the rehabilitation center and do his therapy and be at the meeting to argue for the resort he loves. Something Mayor Bell said to me earlier struck a chord with me. She said Norton would have had a much more difficult time convincing Garrett's neighbors to sign his petition if Garrett had been here and they'd had to look him in the eye. I want to be sure our feed is two-way, so Garrett can see what's is going on here and everyone in the room can see him as well."

"Shouldn't be a problem. We can hook it up so that Garrett can use his laptop as a monitor. I was going to head into town anyway to mail the map you found to my friend at the museum. Come with me and we can stop at the town hall after. Do you still want to show the map to Meg before I send it off?"

"Yeah. It might be a long shot, but I have a feeling the map might lead us to Buck's killer."

At the museum, I postulated the idea that the map we'd found in the attic might be one the town had used at one point for an annual treasure hunt. I asked Meg if she had copies of maps that had been used in the past.

"I do have copies of all of them," she told us. "The originals are in the back, the copies we have on display as part of the island's tourism section."

"Does this look like it could be one of them?" I unrolled the map I'd found and laid it on the counter where we were all standing.

Meg looked at it. She took her time studying it, but, based on her facial expression, she appeared to be confused. "I don't think this is a map from any of the treasure hunts," she eventually said. "In fact, I don't think it's even a map of this island."

"Why do you say that?" I wondered.

"The shape is wrong." Meg walked over to her computer and pulled up a graphic. "The island on the map you found has a sort of a kidney shape, but Gull Island is more of a Q shape."

By Q shape Meg seemed to be referring to the fact that the island was basically round with a narrow peninsula at the bottom, like the letter Q. I could see what she meant though. The island on the map did appear to be shaped like a kidney. Chances were the inlet part was a lovely little bay.

"Of course, if the map was drawn a couple of hundred years ago, as I first suspected, the person who drew it wouldn't have had the advantage of an aerial view," Kyle pointed out.

"True. I suppose the map might simply have been hastily sketched, but if it's showing the way to a treasure I'd say it's most likely buried on this island over here." Meg pointed to a small island well off the coast of the larger one.

"What island is it?" I asked.

"The locals refer to it as Sanctuary Island. It's unpopulated other than the abundant wildlife that live in this area. It's far enough off the beaten track that it receives few visitors, yet it's close enough that you can make the trip there by boat and back in a single day. The island is really more of a mountaintop. The terrain is steep and there's very little beach except right here in the bay." Meg pointed to the inlet. "Most weekenders interested in island hopping head toward this cluster here." Meg pointed to a group of small islands off the coast. "They're also unpopulated, but they have wonderful beaches for anyone looking for a day trip."

I studied the map I'd found and compared it to the shape of Gull Island on the computer screen. Meg was right; it did appear the map could lead to something buried on Sanctuary rather than Gull Island.

"It'd be fun to check it out," I said to Kyle.

Kyle looked at Meg. "How long does it take to get there?"

"It depends on the speed of the boat you're using to make the trip, but I'd say three to four hours. Most of the folks who visit the island do so in boats with cabins so they can anchor and spend the night before heading back. It's worth the trip even if there isn't any treasure there. The variety of birds alone makes it worth your time. And then, of course, there are the turtles, as well as an abundance of sea life."

"It sounds wonderful," I commented.

"Maybe this weekend?" Kyle looked at me. "If I can arrange for a boat rental."

"Sounds like fun."

"If you're really interested, I have a friend who has a fleet of yachts he rents out. They aren't anything elaborate, but I know they all have kitchens and spacious living areas. My college roommates and I rented one two summers ago, and it seemed like it could sleep eight. If the two of you are going alone he has smaller boats as well."

"It might be fun to bring the girls. I don't see Grandpa wanting to make that long a voyage—Doc either, for that matter."

"If you have a number for your friend I'll look into it," Kyle said to Meg.

She jotted down a name and phone number. "Tell Drake I sent you. We go way back. In fact, I was married to him for a brief moment in time."

"Married?"

"Long story."

I wished I had time for that long story, but Kyle and I really needed to get over to the town hall so that everything would be ready in time for the meeting. We thanked Meg and promised to let her know how everything worked out.

* * *

The town hall was empty at that time of day, but I'd called Betty Sue Bell to explain what we wanted to do and she'd arranged to have someone let us in. The room where the meeting would be held was a multiuse space where rows of folding chairs facing toward a stage with a podium and six additional chairs already had been set up. I imagined the chairs could be removed to make way for banquet tables in the event that a meal of some sort would be served, and the podium could be stored if the stage was needed for a performance of some sort.

"This meeting has me feeling nervous," I said to Kyle as he strung wire to hook up the large monitor we'd borrowed from the local library for the evening.

"It's natural you might feel that way, but it seems to me Garrett is still in the driver's seat. Norton seems to know what he's doing and it does seem like he's garnered quite a bit of support, but if you ask me, the idea of invoking eminent domain in this specific situation is probably no more than a threat."

"Do you think he might have something else? A tool we aren't aware of?"

"Like what?"

Kyle walked to the back of the room to check out the angle of the monitor.

"When I spoke to Toby yesterday he mentioned he'd seen Norton at the resort with Buck before he died. When I saw Norton earlier today I asked him about it and he declined to comment. I've been trying to figure out why he would have been at the resort with Buck in the first place. They don't seem like they would have had enough in common to form an alliance of any kind. Then it occurred to me that perhaps Buck knew something that would help Norton and he decided to cash in on that knowledge."

"You're losing me. What could Buck possibly know that would be of value to Norton?"

"I don't know exactly, but we know Buck was after the map and we know he believed Garrett had it, and we suspect he was in the attic looking for the map when he died. But what if that wasn't the case? What if Buck had been in the attic looking for the map on an earlier occasion and in the course of searching for it he came across something else?"

"Something Norton might be interested in?"

"Exactly. I have no idea what; maybe he found a deed or some environmental reports, or even an old will or other document Norton felt he could use against Garrett. There are boxes and boxes of paperwork up there; it makes sense Buck would look through all those boxes for the map."

"So Norton went to the resort with Buck to see what he had," Kyle said.

"Exactly."

Kyle didn't seem convinced. I couldn't really blame him—my theory was really nothing more than a random thought that had taken root the longer I considered the idea.

"Supposing that this scenario is true and Buck really did find something he thought Norton might want, we'll need to figure out what that something is. It could be anything, really. Where would we even start?" Kyle asked.

I leaned against the podium. "I don't know. Maybe the attic where we suspect Buck found the damning evidence in the first place?"

"If there ever was something valuable in the attic we have to assume Norton has it now, so it isn't there anymore. Let's just get through this meeting and take things from there."

CHAPTER 14

By the time seven o'clock rolled around, the room in the town hall was completely packed. The mayor and the other town council members sat on the stage, while Greg Norton and another man in a suit I didn't recognize sat in the first row facing them. Kyle was waiting on the stage near the monitor for the go ahead to dial Garrett in, while I stood off to the side near the door. Apparently Betty Sue had spoken to Garrett on the phone earlier to make him aware of the meeting procedure she would be asking everyone to adhere to.

"I see you made it," I greeted Frank as he walked in.

"I always did love a fireworks show."

"I'm sorry to disappoint you, but you may not be getting the fireworks you're hoping for."

"You aren't going to give up without a fight?"

"Me? No."

"Should be interesting." Frank winked and took a seat.

"If we can all take a seat we'll get started," Betty Sue, who was dressed tonight in a sharp business suit, said into the microphone. As soon as everyone sat, she nodded at Kyle to make the connection. "Because tonight's meeting concerns property owned by Garrett Hanford, we've decided he really should be here." There was an audible gasp as Garrett's face appeared on the screen. "Welcome, Garrett. Can you see us okay?"

"I sure can."

I glanced at Norton, who was whispering something to the man sitting next to him. I smiled at the scowl on his face.

"Before we begin I'd like to go over the rules for tonight's meeting," Betty Sue continued. "I realize that the topic up for discussion tonight has all the ingredients to quickly escalate out of control, but I'm here to tell you that I am not going to let that happen." Betty Sue paused and looked at the crowd, making eye contact with several individuals, including Norton and his guest. "We're going to discuss the matter before us in a civilized manner. Mr. Norton will begin by outlining his plan, after which Garrett Hanford will have the opportunity to respond. Anyone from the audience who would like to comment will be given the opportunity to do so at the appropriate time. Anyone who speaks out of turn or is rude or combative will be removed from the room. Is everyone clear on this?"

Everyone nodded or murmured that they understood.

"Mr. Norton has the floor. Garrett, I'm going to ask that you refrain from responding until after he's finished speaking."

Greg Norton got up in front of the crowd armed with a slideshow, graphs, drawings, and charts. He'd certainly come prepared. I couldn't help but notice the interest on a lot of faces as he showed us drawings of the proposed megaresort. It really looked like a beautiful setup, if you were into that sort of thing. After he got everyone's interest with the drawings and photos he brought out charts that predicted the economic growth the island as a whole would achieve once the megaresort was opened. He emphasized the fact that the increase in the tax base would allow for upgrades to the island's infrastructure: roads, public buildings, community parks, and other common areas. I was forced to admit he'd really done his homework and his presentation was impressive.

When he was finished, the floor was turned over to Garrett. I watched as he seemed to study the faces of the people he called friends and neighbors before he began to speak. "Mr. Norton has put together an excellent presentation," Garrett began. "He has provided some fascinating information and made some interesting promises. While I applaud his efforts, the fact of the matter is that while a megaresort, such as the one his company has proposed, may bring certain things to the island, including a stronger economic base, it will also take away from the island much of what makes Gull Island the sort of place where we've all chosen to live."

Garrett continued to make eye contact with those seated in the front of the room. "We all know that an increase in tourism will drive away the wildlife. I don't think that even needs to be stated. What you all may not have taken into consideration, however, is that a megaresort will change the very nature of our community."

Garrett paused and looked around the room as he let that point sink in.

"I'll return to the idea of the nature of our community in a moment, but first I'd like to address the negative impact that such a resort would have on local business. Mr. Norton talked about the influx of dollars to the local economy, but what he didn't mention was the fact that most of those dollars would be spent at the resort and not at your businesses. How many of you have visited other resorts of the type proposed by Mr. Norton? Of those who have, how many of you have actually left the grounds of that all-inclusive resort from which you'd purchased a lodging and meal package to patronize other businesses in the area?" Garrett paused again for effect. "I'm sure those of you who have vacationed at such properties are realizing that you actually spent very little money outside of the package you'd already paid for."

After another moment, Garrett continued. "And what of the need for employees for this resort? We already have something of a housing shortage. Where are the men and women Norton will need to hire going to live? And with such a large increase in the area's population, how is our current infrastructure going to hold up? Will the additional tax dollars that are brought into the area provide a windfall, or will those dollars be sucked up providing upgrades to roads and utilities and other overloads to our current infrastructure that a resort of that size will create? Furthermore, is it not true that the island already deals with issues regarding water shortages? What do you think a large resort with hundreds of rooms, landscaping, pools, and restaurants will do to this already sensitive issue?"

I looked around the room as Garrett continued to speak. I'd pretty much assumed his plan was to simply state his refusal to sell and leave it at that, but I could see now that he'd taken the time to provide his friends and neighbors with a differing perspective from the one Norton had been presenting to them. Once he'd finished tearing down the plan Norton had presented, he began to present his own plan for the land and his vision for the future.

"Gull Island isn't just a destination; it's a way of life. It isn't just a place to live, it's a place to raise a family. The men and women from whom you buy your groceries and who fix your car when it breaks down aren't strangers who share a zip code; they're friends many of you have known your entire lives. Gull Island is a place where you can step back in time to an era where things were easier. It's this small-town flavor that the visitors who return to us every year are looking for. The world is full of destination resorts, but there's only one Gull Island. It's with those visitors in mind that I want to renovate my resort so that we can continue to attract people with the desire to embrace that which is unique to our history, our culture, and our way of life. The movies on the beach, fireflies in the summer, and turtles nesting along our shore."

As Garrett continued I noticed smiles on the faces of some neighbors who had come to fight. By the time the mayor opened the floor for comments from the audience it was apparent that Garrett had managed to steer the majority of the room to his way of thinking without having to resort to digging in his heels or challenging the desires of those he called friends. I wasn't certain Norton would pack up and go away immediately, but by the end of the meeting I felt confident that Garrett's plans for his resort would find a way to survive.

"Garrett really nailed it," I said to Kyle after the meeting as we took down the equipment we'd installed a few hours earlier.

"Yeah, he really did. And he managed to keep his cool."

"Do you think Norton will go away and find another community to pick on?"

Kyle paused as he wound up the electrical cord. "I'm not sure. All I can say for sure is that Garrett managed to suck the wind right out of his sails."

"I'll go as far as to say that if Buck did dig up something Norton could use in his fight to buy the resort he would have used it here tonight. If that theory didn't hold water and Buck didn't find anything, do you still think Norton could have killed Buck?"

"I honestly have no idea. Do we have any other suspects left?"

"Not many. Toby suggested I might want to consider Digger as a suspect. He didn't seem like a killer when I spoke to him, but Toby told me Digger and Buck had a history of skirmishes that took place whenever Buck decided to dig for treasure too close to a turtle nest."

"I'd be willing to buy that if Buck's body had been found on or near the beach, but why would Digger be in the house?" Kyle and I exited the building and then began loading the equipment into the car.

"I thought of that as well. It doesn't make sense that Digger would be in the attic."

"Do you think we might have narrowed our suspect list too much by focusing on the map?" Kyle asked. "Could there be another reason Buck was in the attic?"

"You mean besides giving something to Norton?" I asked as we returned to the auditorium for the next load.

"Yeah. I'm not sure how we'll be able to prove or disprove that unless Norton admits Buck gave him something or we find evidence that he has something that was known to be in the attic. Can you help me move this table back against the wall?"

Kyle and I picked up the table and returned it to its original location before I continued. "I guess the one thing everyone has said about Buck is that he befriended people easily. It also seems he managed to make some of his newer friends angry on a fairly regular basis. Both Toby and Gil had nothing but negative things to say about him. Toby did tell me Buck lost the map they'd bought together in a poker game. I suppose it's possible Buck was in the attic looking for something to sell if he ended up losing to the wrong people. The attic didn't seem to be a treasure trove of valuable items, but there are some antiques up there that could have value."

"Okay, so if we assume Buck was in the attic to find something of value in general, does that open up our suspect pool?" Kyle asked as we gathered the next load.

"Not really," I answered as we headed toward the car. "The problem is, we never met the man, so we really have no idea who he might have been hanging out with. Although..."

"Although?"

"Blackbeard seems to have a knack for communicating. He continues to repeat the words 'Charlie bad.' What if Blackbeard was in the attic when Buck was killed? Do you think the bird is smart enough to actually name Buck's killer?"

Kyle frowned.

"I don't know. The bird does seem to be smarter than average, but to actually identify a person by name? Have you ever heard him call anyone else by name?"

"He calls you Captain Kyle."

"That's true. But even if he recognized someone named Charlie in the house, the concept of bad versus not bad is pretty advanced for a bird."

"Garrett told me the other day that Blackbeard seemed to understand it."

"We need to ask around to see if there's anyone named Charlie on the island who might have had reason to be with Buck on the night he died."

"Exactly. We'll ask Gertie, Meg, and a few others tomorrow. Garrett already said he didn't know anyone named Charlie when I asked him about it after the first time Blackbeard said it."

"Should we return this stuff tomorrow?" Kyle asked after we finished loading the car.

"Yeah, it's late. We should probably head back to the resort."

I climbed into the passenger seat while Kyle slid in behind the wheel. It was another beautiful night. The air was warm, the stars were bright, and there was a gentle breeze. Even in the middle of summer it was cool after dark at Paradise Lake. I missed my mountain home, but it was nice to mix it up a bit.

"You know, after everything Garrett said about home and hearth I find I'm a little homesick," I commented as we drove.

"Yeah, I had the same feeling. Don't get me wrong, I'm enjoying my time here and am looking forward to the rest of the summer, but I think I'll be ready to go home when the time comes."

"At least you know where home is," I grumbled. "I still haven't made up my mind about where the girls and I should live once we get back to Paradise Lake."

"I doubt your dad plans to kick you out."

"He doesn't. In fact, both he and Rosalie have said we're more than welcome to stay indefinitely. But I have a feeling that when it comes to the needs of a newly engaged couple, more isn't necessarily merrier. I've considered getting an apartment in town for the girls and me, but we have two dogs and three cats between us, so that may not be as easy as it sounds."

"Come and live with me," Kyle said. "I have plenty of room for you and the girls and the animals, and even Ben, if he wants."

I looked at Kyle. "Yeah, you have room, but not enough where we won't be in your way."

"You won't be in my way. I think it would be nice to have other people in the house. Right now it's just me rambling around the place, and it gets lonely at times."

"You hated it when your mother lived with you," I reminded my very generous friend.

"Are you going to pick out my clothes every day and clean out my bedside drawers without asking me?"

"Well, no."

"Are you going to open my mail or throw away the leftover pizza I'd been saving for lunch because I haven't been eating enough vegetables?"

I laughed. "I might. Vegetables are important, but I get your point."

"When my mom lived with me it wasn't that I didn't enjoy having another person in the house; it was more that she treated me like an eight-year-old."

"It's so sweet of you to offer, but I'm afraid a living arrangement like that could ruin our friendship."

"It won't."

"It might."

Kyle shrugged. "It's up to you, but the offer is open and I really hope you'll consider it. You don't have to decide now; take some time to think about it. We *are* basically living together this summer. Let's see how it goes."

I thought about the dreams I'd been having of Kyle and me locked in a passionate embrace. Living with him under the same roof didn't sound like a good idea in the least. "That's fair enough, I guess. And thank you. However it turns out, it means a lot that you offered."

CHAPTER 15

Friday, June 23

The next morning Kyle and I decided to have breakfast at Gertie's after we dropped the girls off at kids' camp. He planned to join the group for their trip to the beach that afternoon, but he had a few hours until they were leaving, so we were using the time to explore our Charlie theory. Gertie's was moderately busy when we arrived, so we took stools at the counter, where we could chat with Gertie while she worked.

"Charlie?" Gertie said as she poured syrup into a small dish. "No, I can't say I know anyone named Charlie."

"What about Charles?" I asked as I buttered my toast.

"No." Gertie shook her head. "Can't think of a single Charles. You know, if you think about it, that's kind of odd. It's not like Charles is a rare name, and we do have a decent population on the island."

"Garrett said the only Charlie he could think of was Charlie Chaplin. Apparently, Blackbeard is fascinated with his hat in the old movies he saw with Garrett. I wonder if that's it. Do you know anyone in town who wears a hat like Charlie Chaplin's? Or even a black hat in general?"

"Can't say that I do. Maybe Blackbeard is referring to some other characteristic, such as the dark suit Charlie Chaplin wears or his bushy dark mustache."

"I guess it really could be anything. For all we know Blackbeard is just rambling."

"What did you think of the meeting last night?" Kyle asked.

"Stroke of genius getting Garrett on camera like that. I definitely get the feeling public opinion shifted after Garrett's speech. Norton might still have a few business owners willing to sign his petition, but not nearly enough to challenge Garrett's right to do as he pleases with his land. My sense is that he and the rest of Destination Properties will move on to the next parcel of land needing to be upgraded."

"I hope that's true, for Garrett's sake. He has enough to deal with without having to worry about them and their megaresort."

"For the most part, folks around here really do want the kind of life Garrett painted. They wouldn't live here otherwise. I think Norton got them to forget that for a bit, but Garrett did a wonderful job of getting them to remember. Can I get you anything else?"

"No thanks. This was delicious. I should get back so I'm not late for my volunteer gig at kids' camp," Kyle informed us.

"I need to pick up Grandpa for our appointment," I added. "Thank you for breakfast."

"It looks like we're back to square one," Kyle commented as we walked out to the car. "If you want to brainstorm after I get back from the beach, I'm in."

"I have softball practice tonight, so it'll have to be after that. I have a feeling we're getting close to figuring this out."

"Really?" Kyle looked at me with an expression of doubt. "If anything, I feel like this is getting more complicated."

"That's how it usually works. Just when nothing makes sense, suddenly everything does."

* * *

After I picked up Grandpa, we headed for our appointment at the Gull Island Senior Home. I wasn't sure why, but my gut told me I'd find the clue I needed to solve the mystery of Buck Barnes's death either at the home or as a result of having gone there in the first place.

I took a moment to look at the grounds as we drove up. The building was lovely, perched on a bluff overlooking the western side of the island, which seemed to attract a lot of wildlife due to the swampy conditions. If I did have a grandparent who was in need of senior care this was exactly the type of place I'd seek out.

"We have care programs for both seniors needing daily medical assistance as well as those who are able to live independently with only a small amount of help," the receptionist informed us. "We're currently at capacity, but we have a waiting list, and we give preference to locals when a room does open up. This is a nonprofit organization, and due to our highly-rated facility and desirable location, we tend to have a lot of interest from seniors looking for a place to spend their final years."

"I'm not in immediate need of a placement, but I might be interested in a spot on the waiting list for my grandfather," I replied. "When I called earlier in the week I was told that if I came back on Friday we could take a tour."

"That's not a problem at all. I'll have one of our volunteers show you around."

The volunteer was a lovely woman named Edith who looked to be in her early sixties. She was both friendly and knowledgeable and made a wonderful first impression.

"It seems you have a lot of volunteers," Grandpa commented.

"There are a lot of caring folks on the island."

"Are all the volunteers seniors like yourself?" I asked.

"No, ma'am. We have volunteers of all ages and all walks of life. The gal who is running the bingo game is the mayor's daughter. She was probably our first volunteer in that age group, but she has managed to recruit quite a few others. There are a couple of volunteers from the church who are in their twenties, and Willow Rivers from the kids' camp volunteers during the winter. Veronica Bolton, the daughter of our local innkeeper, is in her twenties and also a volunteer, as is Frank Davenport, who works at a local bar, and Rory Savage, a nephew of Deputy Savage."

"I heard Deputy Savage helps out here as well," I queried.

"He does indeed. He's one of the best. I'm not sure what we'd do without him. He's always willing to jump right in and help out with our most difficult residents."

I almost felt like Deputy Rick Savage was too good to be true, which should have made me suspicious, but then I remembered the kittens. I was such a sucker for small balls of fur.

"So you take seniors with all sorts of health issues?" Grandpa asked.

"The Gull Island Senior Home was designed to help seniors with a wide variety of needs," Edith informed us. "We have a full-care facility with round-the-clock nursing care as well as independent housing for those who require less assistance."

"What would you say the ratio of those needing daily care to those needing occasional help is?" I asked, because I felt I should be asking relevant questions, not because I really needed to know.

"Our full-care facility has twenty rooms, all of which are filled at all times. We also have independent housing that accommodates up to thirty residents. The condos are one-bedroom units, many of which are filled by a single person, but we do have several couples who live there as well." Edith paused to speak to a woman who was slowly making her way along the path that intersected with the path we were walking on. I had to admire her gumption. Her progress was slow, as she carefully took each step with a cane to help steady her. Suddenly it occurred to me that Charlie Chaplin had a cane.

"Are the residents allowed to come and go as they please?" Grandpa asked.

"Most are. We do have some residents with mental issues that would make it unsafe for them to leave the property without supervision. Those residents are grouped in a special unit with additional security. Residents are allowed to leave the property, of course, but only with individuals who have been designated by the families. If you'll come this way, I'd love to show you our state-of-the-art rehabilitation center."

"Do residents who aren't supposed to leave ever manage to wander off?" I asked.

The guide frowned. "I can assure you that we take the utmost care to prevent that from happening."

"But it has occurred?" I pressed.

"Yes," Edith admitted. "It has. Especially when the resident is aided by well-meaning but uninformed accomplices."

"Accomplices?" I asked.

"I really shouldn't say, but there was an individual who used to do maintenance who didn't always display the best decision making. Not to worry though. He's no longer with us."

Suddenly I wondered if the killer Savage was trying to protect was his own father. I knew Buck used to help out at the home in exchange for the use of a rental owned by Colin Walton. It made sense if she was referring to Buck as the person who'd helped and was no longer with them; naturally because he was dead. I remembered reading in an article that dementia patients could display a variety of symptoms, from loss of memory to an inability to control moods and exercise proper judgment. What if Buck had managed to liberate Rick Savage's father from the home in order to take him on a treasure hunt, but things had gotten out of control? If Savage's father had hit Buck with the cane he used to steady himself, it was entirely possible he wouldn't remember having done so.

"I was hoping to speak to Colin Walton while I was here."

"I'm sorry, but Mr. Walton is unavailable today. If you should decide to place your grandfather with us, I can assure you Mr. Walton will not only meet with you but will happily answer any questions you may have."

"I understand this facility provides for seniors regardless of their ability to pay."

"Yes, that's true. Mr. Walton has worked very hard to set up endowments that help us provide for those who are chosen regardless of their financial situations. Will your grandfather require assistance?"

"Actually, no. My grandfather is quite wealthy." I was curious to see if the prospect of a wealthy applicant might earn me an immediate meeting with Mr. Walton, but it didn't. It really did seem that residents were selected based on criteria that had nothing whatsoever to do with money. On the surface, the home seemed too good to be true, but experience had taught me that if something seemed too good to be true it most likely was.

CHAPTER 16

"Oh, good, you made it." Jack jogged over and gave me a high five when I arrived at the ball field later that afternoon. Well, it was high for me; he actually had to reach down to meet my hand. "We're having a scrimmage, so we need all the help we can get."

"Thank you for inviting me. I'm really excited to get out and get some exercise. Seems like it's been a while since I've had a chance to pound a softball into submission. Where do you need me to play?"

"Rick is the coach, so he assigns positions. Any one you prefer?"

"I can play anywhere. I don't really have the reach for first base, but I can manage. I like to pitch."

"We could use a pitcher."

"You aren't seriously considering letting this teeny tiny girl pitch, are you?" a tall man with a blue shirt and a blue baseball cap asked.

"I'm stronger than I look," I defended myself.

The man snorted.

"Tj, this is John," Jack introduced. "You know how every

school has a bully and every softball team has a jerk? John is ours."

"Happy to meet you, I think."

John spat a wad of sunflower seed shells to a spot just to my left and walked away without responding.

"John is okay once you get to know him," Jack assured me.

"If you say so," I said doubtfully.

"Come on. I'll introduce you to everyone else. I think you'll find we're a fun group."

I felt a rush of adrenaline as I took in the fresh-cut grass, stands full of spectators, and bags of sunflower seeds that were being passed around among team members. It was only a scrimmage, but a surprisingly large number of locals had turned out to watch, which added to the adrenaline rush. Besides, it had been a long time since I'd played for fun. Sure, I occasionally joined in with the girls I coached during practice, but actually being a member of a team made up of my peers hadn't occurred since before my sisters had come to live with me and my life had changed from carefree to complicated.

After Jack introduced me to everyone on both the team I would play for and our opponents, Rick Savage asked me to throw a few pitches to the catcher so he could observe my form. At first I was admittedly rusty, but after the first few pitches I had half the team standing around cheering me on. I pitched a three-inning shutout before everyone changed positions to give those on the bench a chance to play. I went to third base for the second half of the game, and by the time it ended after two hours of play, I found myself asking why I hadn't made more of a point to take time for myself once the girls and I had gotten settled following our mother's death.

"We're going for beer and pizza," Jack informed me.

"Sounds good, but I told my sisters I wouldn't be late. They're still trying to get settled in. Maybe next week?"

"Sure. You did great tonight. In fact, you might singlehandedly be responsible for the first win we've had all season."

"This was your first win?"

"First of many."

"Is there a place I can clean up a bit? That last slide into home covered me in dirt from head to toe."

"Locker rooms are over there." Jack pointed to a building not far away. "By the way, I spoke to Garrett. He seemed interested in my idea of subdividing the property."

I hated to ruin Jack's good mood by telling him I'd had a similar conversation with him, though my understanding concerning his desires was quite different, so I simply told him I couldn't wait to see his plans. He promised to come by Monday as planned. I gathered my things and headed to the locker room. My phone rang just as I neared the entrance. It was Kyle.

"Hey, Tj, are you done with practice?" Kyle asked.

"I am. I just need to wash up and then I'll be home."

"How'd your visit to the senior home go today?"

"Really good, actually. In fact, I think I might have figured this whole thing out."

"Really? Do tell."

I thought I heard someone coming up behind me, but when I turned around there was no one there, so I continued. "It occurred to me that when Blackbeard said 'Charlie bad' he might have been referring to Charlie Chaplin's cane and not his hat as we suspected. I remember seeing a cane in the attic on the afternoon we found Buck's body, but when I looked around the other day it was gone."

"So you think someone hit Buck with the cane?"

"I do. I think that the cane was the murder weapon and Savage knew it, so he removed it from the property when he came back that evening."

"Why would he do that?"

"When I went to the senior home today, the woman who did the tour commented that someone who used to work there had helped someone in the maximum-care facility leave without anyone knowing. What if Buck liberated Savage's father in order to take him on a treasure hunt? We know he has dementia, and it's likely he uses a cane. What if something happened when they were in the attic and Savage's father had an episode? He could have hit Buck with the cane and then forgotten about the whole thing."

"Sounds like a good theory. What are you going to do?"

"I don't know yet. I'll be home in a few minutes. We'll talk about it then."

"We're going to take the dogs for a quick walk," Kyle informed me. "We'll talk when we get back."

I hung up and turned around. Rick Savage was standing in the exit to the men's locker room.

"Interesting theory," he said as he walked toward me blocking my way.

"Is it true?" I demanded. "Are you covering up Buck's murder to protect your father?"

Savage frowned. I waited for I don't know what. He was a cop, so I doubted he'd kill me, but he had gone to a lot of trouble to protect his father, so who knew what he was capable of. Suddenly the rage I had been feeling turned to fear of what was going to happen next.

"Your theory is actually a very good one, but it's only partially correct. It's true Buck managed to check someone out of the senior home to take on his treasure hunt. And it's true I strongly suspect that individual had an episode during the expedition and killed him. It's also true the person in question doesn't remember anything about that day. The individual was found wandering down the middle of the road not far from the senior center, and we all assumed the extent of his unauthorized field trip was limited to the area between the home and the place where he was picked up. I had no idea he actually ended up all the way across town in Garrett's attic until I responded to your call on Monday. The part you have wrong is that it wasn't my father I suspected killed Buck; it was Garrett's."

Color me stunned. In a million years I'd never expected that. "Garrett's? I thought Garrett's father died when he was a baby."

"That's what everyone thought, until I arrested him a while back for petty theft. At the time I arrested him, he seemed confused and told me he couldn't remember his last name. I suspected he was lying until I ran his fingerprints and the name Maxwell Hanford came up. I now believe Max suffers from the same disease as my father."

"Are you sure this Max is Garrett's father?"

"I'm sure. Garrett's father had been arrested for breaking and entering a couple of times during his treasure-hunting days, so his prints were on file."

Wow. Talk about a complicated twist to an already complicated murder. "If Garrett's father is alive, why did his mom lie and tell Garrett and everyone else he was dead?"

"I'm not sure. I suspect Garrett's mom was afraid he'd get caught up in the treasure-hunting fever and didn't want that for her only child, so she simply told Garrett he was dead."

Poor Garrett. I let the idea sink in before I spoke again. "So how did Garrett's father end up back here after all these years?"

"I don't know what brought him back to Gull Island. Like I said, the man seemed confused. At the time of his arrest he knew his first name but not his last, and he didn't remember why he was in the area. I spent some time talking to him, trying to explain to him where he was and, more importantly, who he was. After a bit he remembered the agreement he'd made with his ex to leave the island. He seemed to be scared that he'd violated his agreement and wanted to leave. I didn't feel right about just sending him out into the world, so I talked him into allowing me to check him into the senior home for observation."

I looked off into the distance at the darkening sky. The entire conversation seemed surreal. "Does Garrett know?"

"No. At first Max made me promise not to tell him that he was alive. He's pretty far gone now, and I honestly doubt he'd care one way or the other. I was on the verge of sharing what I knew with Garrett when he had his stroke. I figured he had a lot to deal with already, so I decided to wait until he recovered. I'm really not sure how he's going to take this, especially now."

Talk about an understatement. I suspected Garrett was going to totally freak out. Not only was the dad he believed dead alive, but he'd killed a good friend and, probably worst of all, his mother had lied to him.

"The thing I don't get is, why was Max even with Buck Barnes?" I asked.

"I suspect somehow Buck knew who he was. Maybe he recognized him. Buck was old enough to have lived here when Max did. It seems reasonable that Buck was convinced Max knew the whereabouts of the map he was after. I suspect he recognized him and decided to break him out of the home and take him to retrieve it."

"So Garrett's mother didn't destroy it?"

"Probably not. Chances are that is simply what she told Garrett to keep him from going down the same path as his father and grandfather."

"So you think either Max remembered the map was in the attic and took Buck to the location where he'd left it, or Buck believed the map was in the attic and took Max there in an attempt to get him to reveal the location?"

"Both good theories. At this point I don't have much to go

on. I know Buck was at the home on the day Max was found wandering in the street because one of the volunteers saw him. And I know Buck was killed in the attic, and I suspect, based on the evidence I uncovered at the crime scene, Max is the one who killed him."

"What evidence?"

"Keep in mind I've really only had a few days to put this all together, but when I arrived at Garrett's home on Friday in response to your call, I realized immediately that the body must be Buck. Initially, I didn't realize the trauma to the head was most likely caused by Garrett's father until I saw the cane I'd given him on the floor behind one of the cabinets."

The cane. *Charlie bad.* It suddenly all made sense. We suspected Blackbeard might have been in the attic when the incident occurred. The window had been left open, and Kyle and I had both felt Blackbeard had been living in the attic ever since Garrett was taken away. Blackbeard had seen a man with a cane—a man like Charlie Chaplin—hit Buck Barnes, causing him to fall to the floor and stop moving. If Blackbeard was referring to the incident, it really was amazing. The cane must have been what Deputy Savage came back for.

"You saw the cane and confronted Garrett's father?"

"I did, but he didn't remember anything. He didn't even remember leaving the home. I have no way of knowing what occurred in the attic that day, but as far as I know, Buck and Max were the only two on the premises."

"So you decided to protect him?"

"Bringing Max to justice for Buck's death won't serve any purpose. Buck is dead, and nothing we do will change that. Max doesn't remember what he did; he probably didn't even realize what he was doing at the time. If I report this, there are those above my head who may see things differently. When I realized what happened, I talked it over with Colin and we decided to keep the truth to ourselves. No one ever would have questioned it if you hadn't decided to snoop around."

"What now?"

"I guess that's up to you. You can keep our secret, or you can have Max arrested. He doesn't have long. Chances are he'll die in jail before his case even goes to trial."

"Is he a danger to others?"

"Honestly, I don't think so, but just to be safe Colin has been keeping a close eye on him, and he's only allowed to interact with others when there's supervision."

I was not normally one to let killers go free, but Savage had a point. No good would come from bringing the truth to light. "What are you going to tell Garrett?"

"The truth. Or at least the part of the truth that's necessary for him to know. If you decide to keep Colin's and my secret, I'll simply tell him that his father has been found and leave out the rest."

I thought about Garrett and the man he would only have a limited chance to get to know. I knew in my heart that sometimes seeking justice wasn't justified at all.

CHAPTER 17

The house was empty when I arrived. Even the dogs were out, so the gang must have still been out for their walk. It was already almost completely dark, so I decided to head upstairs to take a shower before the girls returned and used up all the hot water.

I poked my head into the sunroom to check on Blackbeard. He was in his cage, but he hadn't been tucked in for the night. I handed the parrot a treat. "It looks like you were spot on as to who killed Buck."

"Charlie bad, Charlie bad."

"Yes, I know. It's amazing that you understand the concept of bad." I filled Blackbeard's food and water. "You aren't a prince locked in a parrot's body due to some sort of magic spell, are you?"

"Pillage the village."

"Yes, I guess that's what happened to the attic. But you don't have to worry about that now. Nothing bad is going to happen. I believe Deputy Savage and I have come to an understanding."

"Grog and wenches, grog and wenches."

I laughed. "Where did you learn sassy talk like that? I need to head up for a shower, so I'm going to cover you now. Would you like another treat?"

"Who's a good boy?"

"You are. Sweet dreams."

I covered the cage and then went upstairs. I was just gathering clean sweats to change into after my shower when I heard a noise that sounded like it was coming from the attic.

"Kyle?" I called. My inquiry was met with silence. "Grandpa? Anyone?"

I shrugged and was about to continue to the bathroom when I heard the noise again. All the people as well as all the dogs living in the house were out, and I knew Blackbeard was safely in his cage, so I had to assume one of the cats had gotten locked in the attic when we were upstairs earlier in the day. I tossed the clothes onto my bed and headed down the hall to the stairway. I flicked on the light and had begun my ascent when the door to the attic swung open and a figure dressed in black came out of the room. I didn't catch more than a glimpse of the figure before he, or possibly she, barreled into me and sent me falling backwards down the stairs.

"Tj, are you okay?" I opened my eyes to see Kyle staring into my face.

"Kyle? What happened?"

"I was hoping you could tell me. We just got home and found you lying at the foot of the stairs. I swear, my heart stopped for the amount of time it took me to determine you were still alive."

I tried to sit up.

"Just lie back. The ambulance is on its way."

"I don't need an ambulance." I touched my hand to my head. I definitely had a bump.

Doc knelt down next to me and began shining a light into my eyes while Kyle continued to hold my hand. "You were unconscious," Doc informed me. "I want to check for a concussion."

"I'm fine, really. I'm sure I wasn't out for long. Maybe a couple of minutes."

"That's long enough," Doc insisted. He instructed me to follow the finger he put in front of my eyes, as well as answer a few questions. I did so and he let me sit up.

"What happened?" Kyle asked.

"I fell, or more accurately, I was pushed."

"Pushed? By whom?"

I put my hand to my head. Geez, I was going to have a headache. "I don't know. I was getting ready to take a shower when I heard a noise in the attic. I thought maybe one of the cats was accidentally locked inside. I was halfway up the stairs when a figure dressed in black came barreling through the door. He ran straight into me, and before I could react or catch myself in any way, I found myself falling backward down the stairs. The next thing I knew I was staring into Kyle's face."

"Better call Savage," Doc instructed Kyle.

"And while you're at it, call off the ambulance," I instructed. "I'm fine."

Doc nodded at Kyle. I assumed the look was his consent to do exactly as I'd asked.

Doc helped me to my feet and led me into my room, where he sat me in a chair. "We'll cancel the ambulance, but you're going to the hospital for an X-ray."

I opened my mouth to argue.

"No arguments. Head injuries can be serious business."

"Okay," I agreed. "I'll go to the hospital. In a car, where someone waits for me and then brings me home to my own bed."

"Deal."

Kyle came back into the room. "Savage is on his way. Ben

has the girls downstairs, but they're pretty upset. Do you feel up to talking to them for a minute to assure them that you're fine?"

"Yeah. Have them come up."

By the time I'd comforted my sisters and assured them I was going to have a bit of a headache but would otherwise be fine, Savage had arrived. Grandpa took the girls down the hall to get ready for bed while Kyle checked on the dogs, who were more than just a little upset, and I talked to Savage while Doc anxiously watched for any signs of concussion.

"Long time no see," Savage joked. The man was actually nice-looking when he smiled. "Any idea who plowed into you?"

"No. It was all a blur. They had on black clothes and a black ski mask. All I could see were his eyes."

"Color?"

"Brown. I think."

"Height and weight?"

"How am I supposed to know? The guy barreled into me. Besides, I was on the stairs."

"Taller that you?"

"Everyone is taller than me."

"Taller than me?"

I looked at the man standing in front of me. "No, I don't think so. Does it really matter?"

"No," Savage admitted. "I don't suppose it does at this point. I'm going to head up to the attic to look around a bit. I'll have a few more questions for you when I'm done."

"She really should go to the emergency room," Doc said.

"We don't have a hospital on the island," Savage informed Doc. "Nearest one is almost an hour away by car."

Doc frowned. "Are you dizzy?"

"No."

"Blurry vision?"

"No."

"Do you feel nauseous?"

"No."

"Okay, I'll just keep an eye on you, but if you start to experience any of those symptoms you need to let me know."

"Okay."

Kyle helped me downstairs, where I curled up on the sofa while we waited for Savage to complete his investigation of the attic. When I'd left softball practice, I'd been convinced that the case of Buck Barnes's death was closed. Now I wasn't so certain. I couldn't imagine why anyone would break into the attic unless it was to steal something, and the only thing I could think that was worth anything was the map that most people didn't even believe existed.

"Can I get you anything?" Kyle asked as he pulled a blanket I didn't really need over my legs.

"No, I'm fine. Is everyone okay?"

"Yeah, they'll be fine. The girls are shaken up, especially Gracie, so Ben is reading them a story."

"I can hear Echo whining."

"He's shaken up as well. I locked him in the kitchen."

"Best to let him come in and check on me before he breaks down the door." I knew my huge self-appointed protector wouldn't remain contained for long.

Kyle did as I asked. When Echo came into the room, I reminded him to be gentle. He stopped in his tracks, then walked over to the sofa and sat at my feet.

"I'm fine," I assured the large dog. "See, ten fingers and toes."

Echo placed a paw on my leg. I scratched him behind the ears.

"Gracie is feeling sad. Why don't you go up to check on her?"

Echo looked toward the stairs and then back at me.

"It's okay. Go see Gracie."

Echo did as I requested.

"You're really good with that dog," Savage said from his vantage point near the stairs.

"He's been trained in search and rescue, so he knows subtle hand signals. Plus, I swear he understands English."

Savage laughed. "Yeah, my dog does too."

"What did you find in the attic?"

"Whoever broke in knew what he was looking for. The paneling along the back wall was pulled away, but nothing else has been disturbed."

"The map."

"Map?" Savage asked.

I explained about the map we'd found after the last break-in and the fact that we'd sent it away to be dated. "Do you think our thief was Max?"

"No. Even if the fog in his brain had cleared enough for him to have the presence of mind to come for the map, he wouldn't have the physical agility to knock into you and run down the stairs. The poor man barely gets around with a cane."

"But if he left his cane here, how did he get all the way across the island to where he was found after he killed Buck?"

"Good question. There has to be more going on than we thought. Someone else must be involved. It seems there has to be a player we haven't considered."

"Any idea who?" I asked.

"Not off the top of my head. Buck knew a lot of people and he did have a way of pulling you into his fantasy about the treasure. People—even good people—can get so swept up in treasure-hunting fever that they end up making bad decisions. I'm sure I can come up with a list of people who might have been lured into Buck's treasure hunt; the problem is that I really can't think of a single person who would want Buck dead."

"How can I help?" I asked.

"Perhaps after you've rested up a bit you'll remember some small detail about the person who pushed you down the stairs. Even a little thing could help. I'll let you get some rest now, but I'll check back with you tomorrow. In the meantime, if you think of anything, call my cell. If someone other than Max killed Buck, I intend to find out who it was."

CHAPTER 18

Saturday, June 24

I had a restless night in which I seemed to jump between very vivid dreams of Kyle kissing me and long bouts of wakefulness as I tried to make sense of everything that had happened. We didn't know exactly when Buck Barnes had died, but we did know what day he'd gone to see Max. Savage confirmed that none of the locals had seen Buck after that day, so we had reason to suspect his theory that Buck had broken Max out and taken him to retrieve the map was most likely what had occurred.

Initially, we'd believed the two men were alone in the attic, but after the events of the previous evening, we now suspected there had been a third person with the men. This third person, we thought, was most likely the one responsible for returning Max to the spot where he was found; it seemed unlikely he could have walked there on his own. The question was, had Max killed Buck, as we'd initially suspected, or had this third party used Max's cane to kill Buck? And if Buck was already dead, why did the man—or woman—flee prior to securing the map?

"Coffee?" Kyle walked up behind me with a large cup of hot liquid.

"Thanks." I had been unable to sleep, so I'd curled up in a blanket on the back deck overlooking the sea.

"Head still hurt?"

"Actually, it's feeling better. I just have a lot on my mind."

"Can I help?" Kyle sat down in the lounger next to mine. I leaned over and rested my head on his shoulder. It was nice to have someone who was there for me when I really needed him.

"I'm going to tell you something, but you can't tell anyone else. At least not until I figure out what I'm going to do with all this information."

"Okay," Kyle agreed.

"After we visited the Gull Island Senior Home yesterday I got the idea that perhaps Buck Barnes had broken Savage's father out of the home to help with his treasure hunt, and that perhaps something had gone wrong and Savage's father had killed Buck."

I went on to explain that residents of the high-security unit did at times manage to sneak away, and given Savage's father's condition, he might not have even known what he'd done. Kyle agreed that this theory would explain why Savage was covering up the murder. When I then told him I'd confronted Savage the previous evening and found out that I'd only been partially correct and it was actually Garrett's father I now suspected of killing Buck, he was as shocked as I had been.

"Wow. That's some story."

"I know. I couldn't believe it when Savage explained it to me. Unfortunately, there are a lot of unanswered questions, due in part to the fact that almost everyone in the know is either dead or suffering from dementia."

"Okay, so if Buck is dead and Max is basically an invalid, who plowed you down last night?"

"That's what I've been trying to figure out. It's totally possible Buck had an accomplice; we just aren't sure who it could be. Initially I assumed that if he had an accomplice it wouldn't be a local because the locals knew Buck well enough not to get pulled in his schemes. But what if he managed to convince someone that the man who had last been seen with the map had returned to the island and with a little help he thought he could get him to give it up? Couldn't that be enough to get someone to take a few hours out of their day to find out if Buck was really on to something?"

Kyle took a sip of his coffee. "I guess that makes sense. He did manage to get Adam Joyner to take leave from his job to help him. You don't think the man you saw was Adam?"

"No. He had the wrong build."

"What did you recognize about the man? Heavy? Thin? Tall? Short? Anything?"

"I've been thinking about that a lot," I assured Kyle. "It all happened so fast that I didn't have time to think then, but I'm pretty sure now that my attacker was a male of average height and weight. I know that doesn't narrow things down at all. Savage said the paneling on the back wall of the attic was pulled away, so the person knew exactly where to go to look for the map. If they'd found the map the night Buck died, why not take it then? Cuervo found the flaw in the paneling which led me to find the map, and it was obvious it had been tampered with. It seems as if someone found the map, put it back, and then went back for it last night. The problem with that theory is that it makes no sense from a time management standpoint."

"It really doesn't. Even if he didn't take the map with him for some reason on the night Buck died, he had plenty of opportunities to go back for it before we arrived. It makes no sense to wait until there was a house full of people."

I took a deep breath and closed my eyes. I leaned my head

back and listened to the sound of the waves. Kyle was right. The person who'd barreled into me last night must have just found out about the map, but how was that even possible? Buck Barnes was dead and Max was safely tucked away in the senior home. Only people who were authorized to do so had been able to speak to him since he'd been returned after he managed to wander away.

"More coffee?" Kyle asked.

"Yeah, thanks."

Echo put his head in my lap as I continued to listen to the waves. I was so incredibly tired. I knew that between the slight headache that lingered and the fact that I'd gotten little to no sleep the previous night, I was going to have a hard time getting through the tasks I'd assigned myself for the day. Not that I had anything all that urgent to attend to. One of the nice things about living on Gull Island for the summer was that my list of responsibilities had decreased enormously. If I were home at Paradise Lake, I'd most likely spend the day helping out at the resort and planning the big Fourth of July blowout we held each year.

"Yo ho, me hearties."

I opened my eyes.

"Blackbeard?"

"He was awake when I went in for the coffee, so I brought him out." Kyle had tied him to a perch that had been set up on the deck for just that purpose.

I smiled. It was sweet the way Kyle doted on the bird. "Good morning to you as well, Blackbeard. I hope you slept well. I'm surprised we didn't wake you with all the commotion."

"Grog and wenches, grog and wenches."

Kyle laughed. "Where did you learn that?"

"That's what I asked him last night. I suppose he could have picked it up from a movie or maybe the person who owned him before Garrett. Garrett doesn't seem like a grog-and-wenches type of guy."

"This is the first parrot I've ever really had any exposure to, but he seems really smart."

"Yeah. I mean, the whole 'Charlie bad' thing turned out to be really true. I wonder what other clues are buried in his little mind." I turned and looked at Blackbeard. "Did you see who was in the attic the day Buck died?"

"Charlie bad, Charlie bad."

"Did you see who was in the house last night?" Kyle added.

"Grog and wenches, grog and wenches."

"I wonder if that's a clue," I commented to Kyle. "Maybe I should call Garrett to see if he knows what it means."

"Good idea. It's a little early yet, but maybe in a couple of hours."

Kyle made a wonderful breakfast for the entire clan, and then I went upstairs to call Garrett. I felt like we were getting close to something; I just didn't know what. Maybe Garrett had some insight he wasn't even aware of.

"Morning, darlin'. How are things on Gull Island?"

"Things are good. It's a beautiful day, although I think it might be cooler than it has been. Before I forget, I wanted to congratulate you on your very persuasive performance on Thursday. I haven't spoken to a lot of people yet, but the ones I have chatted with seem to think Norton will roll up his blueprints and go away."

"Glad to hear it. I'm not really in a position to deal with a big legal battle."

"I assume you want to continue with the renovations?"

"I do. Jack sent over his drawings."

"And...?"

"And although they're very well thought out, I would still prefer to sell to a single owner who will run the place as a small family resort."

"Did you tell him that?" I asked.

"Not yet, but I will." I could hear depression mixed with resignation in Garrett's voice. "In the meantime, don't say anything. I don't want to leave him with the impression I came to a decision without giving his idea fair consideration."

"I won't say a thing," I promised. I had two practices next week with Jack for the softball tournament, so I just hoped it wouldn't come up. I was a pretty lousy liar; if put in the position in which even a white lie was necessary, I'd usually fidget and hem and haw. A dead giveaway, or so those who knew me well had assured me.

"How's Blackbeard doing?"

"Really well. He has a new saying I'm curious about: 'grog and wenches.' He's repeated it several times."

Garrett laughed. "I take Blackbeard to Sully's with me sometimes. Frank always has a treat for him and the locals get a kick out of him, so he loves to go. When we first pull up to the bar he always says 'grog and wenches.' I'm not sure how that started, but everyone gets a laugh out of it."

The bar. Now that I thought about it, it did seem as if my attacker last night had had the stench of beer on him. Could it have been someone who had been in the bar prior to coming out to the house? If so, maybe whoever was tending bar would know which of their patrons had spilled beer on himself the previous evening.

"I must say, Blackbeard is the smartest bird I've ever seen."

"He is. Did you know he was the one who called for help when I had my stroke?"

Garrett has an old corded phone in the kitchen. "He can dial a phone?"

"No, but he can knock the handset off the receiver and peck at my speed-dial buttons. He happened to call Rick, although even I don't think that was intentional. When Rick answered, he said, 'Man overboard,' and Rick came running."

"That's amazing."

"It really is. Blackbeard is a special bird. I'm glad he's at home and you're willing to take care of him. It means a lot."

"I'm more than happy to do it. He's really something special and everyone is having a wonderful time with him, with the exception of my cat Cuervo, who isn't fond of him in the least. Are things going well with your therapy?"

"It's going okay, but I have to admit that even though the circumstances weren't ideal, seeing everyone via video feed the other night has made me even more homesick than I was. This damn stroke has really made a mess of things."

"I'm so sorry. I know this must be hard on you."

"I hate to complain, but it really has. Not only do I miss Blackbeard and all my friends, but I haven't been outside of this darn center in days. After a while it gets pretty depressing."

"Don't they have nurses who'll take you outside for some fresh air?"

"Sure, there are nurses who will take you out. In a wheelchair. I can walk just fine. I don't need to be wheeled around in a chair. Damn nurses want to coddle me like I'm a babe in swaddling."

"You did have a major stroke," I reminded him.

"No need to remind me. My body does that every day."

I wanted to say something comforting, but the reality was that Garrett was going through a major life change that would most likely leave him with permanent disabilities for the remainder of his life. It must be a very hard reality to come to grips with.

"Have you thought about transferring to the Gull Island

Senior Home? It seems like you could get the care you need and be near the people you care about."

"I may be an invalid, but I'm not a senior. I just turned fifty-eight on my last birthday."

"Do they have an age requirement?"

"No. Not really. Colin called me early on and we chatted about it. At the time, I told him I wasn't a fan of the idea because I'd be the youngest one in the whole place, but he said there were advantages to being close to folks I know. Guess he might have a point, but I'm still having a hard time wrapping my head around the idea that I may never be able to live on my own again."

"I can't imagine what you're going through and I'm certainly not suggesting I'm in a position to offer you advice, but I'm sure your friends would welcome the opportunity to spend time with you, and I'd be willing to bet that not one of them would think any less of you for being in a wheelchair."

Garrett didn't answer right away, but it seemed as if he might be considering the situation. When he did reply, he changed the subject, leading me to believe he needed more time to consider his options.

"I need you to make sure that Jack knows that the cabins closest to the turtle eggs aren't to be touched until after hatching season. We don't want to disturb the little darlings."

"I'll tell him, and I know Digger has been keeping an eye on the nests and I will as well. The turtles are in good hands."

"Thank you, darlin'. It looks like it's time for my therapy. Let's talk again soon. It helps pass the time to listen to your cheerful voice."

I didn't feel like the conversations I'd had with Garrett to date had been particularly cheerful in nature, but if he found comfort in them, I'd make a point to call him every day.

CHAPTER 19

After I finished speaking to Garrett I headed into town. He'd said Blackbeard referred to Sully's as "grog and wenches," and so far the bird had been spot on, so I figured it was worth it to talk to Sully. I doubted the bar would be open that early, but perhaps Sully would be around and would know who might have taken a beer bath the previous evening. Luckily for me, there was a delivery truck unloading supplies through the alley entrance, so I let myself in to the bar through a back door. The only person there, however, was Frank, who was speaking with the delivery guy and hadn't seen me come in. I waited while he completed his conversation.

"It's been real nice working with you," the delivery driver said. "I'm sorry to see you go."

"I never intended to work here for more than the few months it would take to earn bus fare west, but things happen, if you know what I mean. Guess it turned out okay though; I was here long enough to buy an old car to get around in, so no more buses for me."

"I'm not a fan of the bus myself. Hopefully your new ride will get you to where you want to go. What direction you heading?"

"West. Don't even have much of a destination in mind, just as long as it isn't here. Can't say I'll miss the place. Hanging out with drunks all day gets old real fast. Worked the day shift yesterday and some guy was so smashed by five o'clock that he dumped his entire glass of beer on me. Luckily, I had a fresh shirt to put on."

Frank? No. He was such a nice guy, although he was sounding a bit less than nice at the moment. He had admitted to knowing Buck. Could they have teamed up?

"Well, good luck with your venture." The delivery driver set the invoice on the counter and reclined his hand truck in preparation to depart. "I'm sure Sully will miss you."

"He'll survive."

After the deliveryman had gone I debated whether to continue on inside to speak to Frank or sneak out and regroup. I was leaning toward leaving and returning later when Frank's phone rang.

"Yeah?" Frank walked over to the bar with his phone to his ear, poured a shot of whiskey, and downed it. "No, I didn't get it. A whole month of kissing up to the old guy and when I finally got him to talk, he sent me on a wild goose chase. I'm beginning to think Buck's treasure really was the myth everyone said it was. Talk about a waste of time. Guess I'm headin' out today. Managed to buy myself a car, so the traveling will be a lot faster than expected. It's a junker, but it runs."

I watched as Frank poured himself yet another shot.

"No. The deputy hasn't figured out that I was the one who hit the guy, but I'm sure it's only a matter of time, which is why I'm heading out while I still can. I'll call you when I get there."

Frank had killed Buck? I was trying to make sense of what I'd heard when I decided it was time for me to go. Unfortunately, I tripped over a discarded beer bottle, alerting Frank to my presence.

"Who's there?" Frank called after he downed the second shot.

I stood perfectly still. I could feel my heart pounding as I waited for Frank to find me or not.

He did.

"What are you doing here?"

"Just saw the door open and stopped by to say hi, which I've done, so see ya."

"Hang on a minute. How long have you been standing here?"

I tried for a light and airy tone, but I suspected the panic I felt was evident in my voice. "Not long. I just got here. Really. So like I said, I'll be going."

Frank grabbed my arm. "What's your hurry? You wanted to pay me a visit, so let's visit. Want a drink?"

"No thanks. I really have to go."

"Sorry, dear, but you ain't going anywhere. I'm not sure if you heard anything, but I can't take that chance."

"Are you going to kill me?"

"Of course not. I'm just going to lock you in the walk-in refrigerator. Don't worry. It's cold but not freezing. Sully will be by in a bit to open up for the afternoon and will let you out, but I'll be long gone by then."

"Wait."

Frank paused.

I realized I needed to stall. I wasn't sure what time Sully would be in, but I did know the less time in the refrigerator the better. "Maybe I will take that drink."

"Too late, sweetheart. Now move it."

"Why are you doing this?" I tried to free myself of his grasp while he pulled me toward the kitchen.

"Like I said, I need time to get off the island, and I suspect your little visit may have to do with more than just a friendly stop-in. I wondered if you recognized me last night. I thought not, but I can see I was wrong."

Frank opened the door to the cooler.

"Can you at least tell me what you were doing in the attic?"

"I was looking for the map. I figured you knew that."

"I did. Sort of. What I don't know is how you knew where to look. Did Max find it on the night you killed Buck and you waited to retrieve it for some reason?"

"No, Max didn't find it. And now I know there was nothing to find. I checked last night and the hiding spot was totally empty. I should have known Buck was full of baloney. Now get in there."

Frank shoved me inside. It didn't seem that cold. Yet. I knew that would change.

"The least you can do is tell me how you got hooked up with Buck."

"Now why should I do that?"

I didn't have an answer for him, but I still felt motivated to stall. I really didn't want him to close that door. "Please? If I'm going to die in here, you may as well assuage my curiosity."

Frank tossed me a sweater. "You aren't going to die. Sully will be here in an hour. But for reasons even I can't explain, I like you, so I'll tell you. Like I said when we met, Buck and I were friends. I took this job intending only to stay for a few months, but near the end Buck and I were chatting while he was helping clean up and he saw some guy come into the bar and went berserk. When I asked him about it, he said the man who'd just come in was a ghost. The guy didn't look dead to me, but I played along and asked him whose ghost we were looking at. He said Max Hanford. He went on to tell me about the treasure map the man supposedly had, and that he'd died while looking for the treasure. Max only stayed for one drink and then left, but Buck and I devised a plan to track him down and make him tell us where the treasure was. Problem was, the guy got arrested, and the next thing we knew he was checked into the old folks' home."

"Where you didn't have access to him."

"Exactly."

"So you decided to volunteer at the home as a means of gaining access to Max."

"You're a smart one. That's exactly what I did, and it worked. It took a while, but eventually I was left unsupervised with the residents in the high-security unit."

"So you helped Buck break Max out of the home and then demanded he lead you to the treasure."

"Bingo. Problem was, when we got to the attic the guy had this blank stare on his face. He didn't seem to remember where the treasure was, or even where *he* was. Buck and I tore the place apart looking for it, but there was nothing. The longer Buck looked, the madder he got. Eventually he grabbed Max's cane out of his hand and threatened to hit him with it. I'm not sure what happened exactly, but the next thing I knew I had the cane in my hand and I smacked Buck with it. I didn't mean to kill him. In fact, I was aiming for his arm, but he turned at the last minute. I grabbed Max and hightailed it out of there."

"And then you left him on the road."

"No. I took him back to the home and told everyone I found him on the road."

Okay, that at least made sense. Frank was a well-liked volunteer; no one would question his assertion that he'd found Max wandering around.

"So why did you stay? Why not leave the island then?"

Frank shrugged. "At the time I really thought Max knew where the map was, so I figured I'd hang out a while longer to see if I could get him to talk. No one knew Buck was dead. Everyone just thought he was off on some extended treasure hunt. I knew Garrett wasn't coming home anytime soon, so I thought I had time. I didn't know about you."

"And yesterday Max finally told you about the map?"

"Yeah. He just blurted it out. It was the strangest thing. One minute he was talking nonsense about seagulls and turtle eggs and the next he was telling me the map was in the wall. 'Course, once I got to the house and went to the wall panel I realized it wasn't there. The whole thing was most likely a scam. What a waste. I could really use a treasure."

If Cuervo hadn't found the map, chances were Frank would have. I had to wonder who'd accessed the map in the first place. It seemed as if neither Buck nor Frank knew what the map led to, and Max had been out of sorts since he'd been here. Or had he?

"Did Max remember that you killed Buck?"

"No. He didn't remember that day at all. I tried to talk to him about it a few times, but he just looked at me blankly or reminded me that he didn't like broccoli. Not that I'm in charge of the meals the residents receive, but I guess I was around often enough that he figured I could talk to the kitchen."

Frank started to close the door.

"Wait. You don't have to do this."

"Yeah, I'm afraid I do."

"Please. I'm really scared." I looked frantically around the refrigerator. "What if Sully doesn't show or he comes in late for some reason?"

"Don't worry, you'll be fine. Even if Sully is late, you're wearing enough clothing to stay warm for quite some time. Now I really do need to get a move on. It's been nice knowing you."

With that, he closed the door.

The worst part wasn't the cold, at least not yet; the worst part was the dark. I pulled out my cell, but there was no reception. At least I had some light until the battery died. I tried to jimmy open the door to no avail. Frank had locked it from the outside. I looked around, although I didn't expect to find a means of escape. It was a refrigerator; there would be no reason to provide a back door or alternate escape route.

I just hoped Sully wasn't late for his shift. I wondered if he'd even come in to the kitchen when he first arrived. It was over three hours until the bar actually opened, so he wouldn't have any reason to begin preparing the food that was served. I decided I'd bang on the door every fifteen minutes. If Sully didn't open the refrigerator door for some other reason, surely he'd hear the banging.

After my first moments of panic I decided to conserve my energy. I found a space near the door and sat down on the floor. I wrapped the sweater around me, and once I was settled, I turned off my phone. I wished now that I'd thought to make sure it was fully charged that morning, but in all the confusion I'd forgotten to plug it in the night before. Now less than 50 percent of the battery was left.

My natural inclination as I sat in the cold dark chamber was to panic, but I knew that would do me no good. Frank was most likely correct. I probably wouldn't freeze before Sully arrived to set me free, even if he didn't find me until opening time. I needed a diversion, so I forced myself to calm my mind and think pleasant thoughts.

I wondered how my dad was doing without Grandpa, the girls, and me. I was certain he was happy to have time alone with Rosalie, but we'd all lived together for quite some time. I wondered if he found the quiet welcome or depressing. Of course, given my mood swings in the weeks before we'd left to come East, I had to assume he was grateful for the break.

I really had taken Jake's death hard. Probably harder than anyone other than Hunter. I'd known Jake my whole life; in many ways he'd been like a second grandfather to me. When he'd died, a hole had been created in my heart that I didn't think I could ever fill. I still thought about him from time to time. His kind smile and ornery nature was definitely a unique combination. I shed a few tears for Jake as I tried not to let my mind wander to thoughts of Hunter. I knew we were better off as friends, but there was a part of me that mourned for what might have been.

I clicked on my phone. Had it really only been ten minutes? I stood up with my back to the wall and pounded on the door. "Sully!" I screamed as loudly as I could.

I continued with this pattern for over an hour. I'd sit on the floor and ponder my life and then take a break to pound on the door and scream the name of the bar owner. I was glad I had my phone to track the passage of time. Otherwise, I feared I would have gone crazy from not knowing.

When one hour turned to two I felt myself become drowsy. I knew it was best not to lose myself in sleep, but the air seemed stale and the urge to close my eyes was becoming stronger. Where was Sully anyway? The bar would open soon. Surely he must be on the premises by now to set up for a busy Saturday night.

The more time that passed the harder I found it to breathe. Were refrigerators air tight? Probably. I stood up and pounded on the door. I knew I should conserve air but I had an overwhelming urge to hyperventilate. I glanced at my phone once again. If Sully didn't show up until the time the bar actually opened I might not freeze but I'd probably suffocate.

I curled myself into a fetal position and willed my breath to slow. I tried to focus on extending the time between breaths but that just made me want to breathe all the more. I tried not to panic but somehow panicking seemed to be the only logical response to the situation.

I felt myself become more and more light headed. I was

afraid I was going to pass out. I knew that I needed to stay awake but if I was going to suffocate maybe drifting into unconsciousness would be the best thing. I squeezed my eyes shut as tears streamed down my face. I tried not to think about how my death would affect my dad and the girls but somehow that was the only thought that dominated my mind. They say that when you die your life flashes before you but as I drifted into unconsciousness all I could see was Kyle. My heart ached with the knowledge that he would never know how very much he really meant to me.

The next thing I knew the door opened and Sully gasped.

"What are you doing here?"

I tried to stand up, but my legs wouldn't work. "Frank. You have to call Savage. Frank killed Buck."

The next thirty minutes were sort of a blur. Sully got me out of the refrigerator and wrapped me in a blanket. He called both Savage and Kyle, who came immediately. Savage was most interested in what I knew about where Frank had gone and what kind of car he'd been driving, while Kyle simply wanted to be sure I was okay. After a bit, Savage agreed it was best that Kyle take me home. He promised to keep us updated as the search for Frank progressed.

"Better?" Kyle asked as he wrapped yet another blanket around me. It had been several hours since he'd brought me home, but I still was having a hard time staying warm.

"Yeah, I'm fine."

I tucked the blanket up to my chin.

"It's a good thing Sully showed up when he did. You really had very little air left."

"You know, I really don't think Frank thought of that. I don't think he wanted to kill me, just detain me. He even gave me a sweater." I looked at the now fully charged phone in my hand. "I wonder if Savage has caught up with him yet."

"When I spoke to him he said he had the state police on it. He said he'd call if he heard anything. Frank had a head start, but unless he changed cars, the beater he was driving should be easy to find. I'm sure they'll catch up with him eventually."

Echo was lying next to me with his head in my lap. He'd been with me the whole time since I'd been home. It was like he knew I'd appreciate the extra body heat.

"How did your conversation with Garrett go?" Kyle wondered.

"It went well. I wasn't sure how all of this was going to affect him, but it seems like he's gone from being depressed about his life to being hopeful about what the future might bring."

"How did he take the news that his father is alive?"

"He was shocked, of course, but he seemed happy to have a chance to spend some time with the man he thought had been dead all these years. Garrett called Colin Walton about trying to arrange a visit and Colin agreed to pick him up and bring him to the island. When Garrett showed up, Max seemed to wake up as if from a deep sleep and he remembered everything. They called Savage, who wanted to get as much out of Max as he could in case he slipped away again. Garrett told me that he'd have Savage call me when he got a chance."

I looked down at my phone, which had buzzed while I was speaking to Kyle. I frowned when I didn't recognize the number, but I answered it anyway.

"Tj Jensen."

"It's Deputy Savage."

"Sorry. I didn't recognize the number."

"I'm calling from one of the offices at the senior home. I wanted to let you know highway patrol just picked up Frank."

I smiled. "Good. I'm glad. How are things going with Garrett and Max?"

"So far so good. Garrett seems like a new man all of a sudden, and Max remembers almost everything. I guess when he first came into town he went out to the house to check on the map. He said it was still in the wall where he'd left it all those years ago. He decided that was as good a place as any, so he left it there and went into town for a drink. He doesn't remember anything after that. That's the way the disease Max has works. One minute the person you're speaking to can be detached from reality as we know it and the next he's right there with you."

"It'll be nice if his alertness hangs around for a while. Now that Garrett and Max have been reunited, it would be a shame if his father drifted away before they have a chance to really catch up on all the years they've missed."

"Colin has arranged for Garrett to move into the Gull Island Senior Home, so Max and Garrett can spend as much time together as they want. I really think that's the best thing for him anyway."

"That's nice."

"I told Garrett I'd arrange for someone to bring Blackbeard by for a visit. They don't allow pets to live on the premises, but they do allow them to visit in the outdoor garden area."

I glanced at the bird, who appeared to be listening to my end of the conversation. I wondered what would happen to him in the long run. As far as I was concerned, he was welcome to stay with us as long as we were on the island, but I wasn't sure he'd like the alpine climate of Paradise Lake.

"Did Max know what the map I found led to?" I asked.

"No. He said he inherited it from his father, who never shared with him what, if anything, he'd discovered."

"I wonder if Max would care if we followed the clues to see where it leads."

"Actually, Garrett said for me to tell you to call him. He said it's very important. I'll give you the number to his direct line. You can ask him about the map when you talk to him."

"Okay, great."

Savage recited the number, which I wrote down. Then we said our goodbyes and I hung up.

"From your end of the conversation it sounded like there was good news all around," Kyle commented.

"There really is. I have to call Garrett, but then I'll catch you up."

Garrett sounded thrilled both to have a chance to get to know the father he'd thought was dead and to be home on Gull Island. I arranged to bring Blackbeard by the following day and he shared that he was looking forward to visiting with both of us. He told me both he and Max were fine with us taking the map to Sanctuary Island to see what we could find there. I promised to fill him in after our trip.

Garrett had saved the biggest piece of news for last. It seemed Max had a daughter, a half-sister he'd never known existed. He'd spoken to her, and he thought she might be willing to take over the resort on a permanent basis. I promised him I'd hold off on the remodel until I heard from him for sure.

"Sounds like more good news," Kyle observed.

I filled him in on everything I'd learned from both Detective Savage and Garrett.

"I can still look into renting a boat if you want to try to go check out the island."

"I'd like that very much."

CHAPTER 20

Wednesday, June 28

As it turned out, everyone wanted to go along for the adventure to Sanctuary Island, so Kyle rented a boat big enough for the entire family plus Meg, who came prepared with a folder full of maps of the island from differing perspectives. We'd decided to make it an overnight trip, so Willow had agreed to stay at the house with Blackbeard and the cats. We brought the dogs with us.

The boat Kyle had rented was really a yacht, so we were required to anchor offshore and then shuttle everyone to the beach via a motorized dinghy.

"Do you think we'll really find a treasure?" Gracie's eye sparkled with enthusiasm as the dinghy landed on the island with the first group, consisting of Kyle as the driver and Ashley, Gracie, the three dogs, and me as the passengers.

"Maybe. We won't know until we look."

"I hope the treasure is made up of beautiful jewels," Ashley added with a gleam in her eye.

"I like jewels," Gracie said.

"Wait right here on the beach," Kyle instructed after we unloaded and he turned the boat around to returned for Ben, Doc, and Meg.

Ashley and Gracie played in the surf with the dogs while I looked around at my surroundings. As Meg had described, the island only had a small amount of beach while the rest consisted of a fairly large mountain smack dab in the middle. According to the map, it looked like we'd need to hike at least partway up the mountain. I hoped the hike wouldn't be too much for the older folks.

By the time we'd managed to shuttle everyone to shore, my grandfather declared he was already exhausted. After a bit of discussion, it was decided that he, Doc, and Meg would wait on the beach with the girls while Kyle and I made the hike up the mountain to see if there was anything to find. Kyle's friend had called the previous day to let us know that the map was around one hundred and twenty years old. Impressive, but definitely not old enough to be Barkley's treasure.

"I'm glad the others decided to wait. This is a steep climb." I wiped my brow with the back of my arm. There was no trail to speak of, but the maps Meg had brought along helped us narrow things down to a meadow of sorts about halfway up where we believed the treasure must be buried.

"It's occurred to me that the map we found could have been drawn to mark the location of something else entirely," Kyle added.

"True. We found a map and immediately thought treasure, but it could be directions to a meeting place or a settlement or an old gravesite." I stopped walking and looked back. Standing on the side of the mountain led to an unobstructed view clear to the horizon. "I suppose it also could have been directions to a lookout. Will you look at that view?"

"It's pretty amazing," Kyle agreed.

I took several deep breaths and then we continued to climb. I was in pretty good shape because I was active in sports and ran on a regular basis, but this was becoming difficult even for me.

"Have you decided what you want to do once Garrett's sister arrives?" Kyle asked.

"Not really." Garrett had called the previous day to let me know that he'd worked things out with the woman, who was due to arrive on August 1st. He'd definitely decided not to sell the resort or even to renovate it at that point. Of course, he let me know we were welcome to stay for as long as we wanted, but given everything that had happened I was seriously considering the possibility of just heading home. "Jenna left a message on my voicemail earlier letting me know that she and the girls are definitely coming for a visit. They arrive on July 10th and plan to stay for two weeks, which will work out great since they will have gone home by the time Garrett's sister arrives. I want to be sure she gets settled okay, but after that I think maybe we'll head back to Paradise Lake. I can't really see a reason to stay. What do you think?"

"Hey, this is your party. I'm just along for the ride."

"Watch out." I stepped over a large rock onto an area with loose shale that caused a mini avalanche. "Are you okay?" I turned around and looked at Kyle, who had been hiking behind me.

"I'm fine. Watch your step though." Kyle looked at the steep climb beneath us. "It wouldn't be fun at all to fall from this height."

"I'll be careful." I found myself wishing I'd thought to wear a hat. There was very little shade on this side of the island at this time of day. "It shouldn't be too much farther until the trail levels off. Maybe a half mile, if Meg's map is correct. Once we get there we can find some shade and take a break."

"Do you really think we'll find a treasure?" Kyle asked.

"I don't know. I hope we do. It would be fun and romantic to dig into the soil and find something that was buried by someone who lived over a century ago."

"We only brought a folding camping shovel, so I hope whoever hid the treasure didn't bury it too deep," Kyle pointed out.

We had been somewhat limited in the size and number of tools Kyle and I could carry up the mountain on our backs, but I figured we could always come back if it seemed there was something to find if we went deeper.

"It looks like the shelf is just up ahead," I called back, hoping it wasn't a false top. Luckily, it wasn't; the trail opened onto a beautiful flat meadow. It was somewhat protected by the mountain that surrounded it, which made it a perfect place, in my opinion, to set up a camp or to bury a treasure.

I sat down in the shade on a flat rock and took a long drink of the water we'd brought. Kyle did the same, and then we opened the map and looked at the markers. At first nothing really looked similar. Of course, it had been over a hundred years. A lot could have changed.

"Whoever drew this map did a very rudimentary job," Kyle observed. "It sort of looks like this pattern of lines matches the rock formation on the mountain over there."

I looked to where Kyle was pointing. The lines were drawn flat on the page rather than in three dimension, which would lift them off the ground onto the side of the mountain, but Kyle was right; it did look like the lines drawn on the map and those etched into the mountain were the same.

"So that would put us here."

I pointed to a spot on the map.

Kyle and I both spent several minutes looking down at the map and then around at our surroundings. It appeared as if the spot designated with an X was slightly to the left of us, near what looked to be a waterfall. Problem was, there was no waterfall.

"Maybe it was just really wet that year, creating a waterfall that has since dried up," I suggested.

"I guess we can walk in that direction to see if we can identify a small stream that might have at one point been a waterfall," Kyle said.

We each took another sip of our water before continuing.

"You know, this meadow is a fair size and pretty unobstructed by trees. We could have just chartered a helicopter to bring us here," I pointed out.

"What would be the fun in that?"

"Maybe you're right, but if we find a treasure chest full of gold or jewels that's exactly how we're getting it out of here. There's no way I'm carrying it down the mountain."

"Agreed."

We walked a while longer and did find a small stream that was really no more than a trickle. Still, Kyle pointed out that the rocks behind the spot where it meandered down the cliff face were worn, as if there had been a greater force of water at some point.

"Okay." I stood still and looked back at the map. "If this is the waterfall the treasure should be there." I pointed to a small crack in the rock's surface.

The bushes that had grown up in the area were both tall and thorny, so we spent the next thirty minutes trying to clear a path to the cliff behind without scratching up our arms and legs.

"I'm starting to think a cold shower and an even colder beer might be more desirable at this point than anything we might find here," I commented as sweat trickled down my back and between my breasts.

"A cold shower does sound good. I wonder if this little stream empties into a pool before it meets up with the sea."

I turned and looked in the direction the water flowed. "Maybe. If it does, it must be on the other side of the meadow. After that the water would flow down the mountain toward the sea. We can look on our way back. If there is water, I'm taking a dip. I can't remember the last time I was this dusty and sweaty."

"I think I see something," Kyle said as he continued to pull the shrubbery away from the cliff face.

"Well, I'll be." The small crack in the cliff became significantly wider at the base. It was large enough for a person to slip into. "Do you think they hid the treasure in a cave rather than underground?"

"Maybe. Do you want to look?"

Did I! "Hell yeah. I'm glad we brought flashlights."

"I'll go first. You stay close behind me. And watch where you step. We have no way of knowing if the floor drops off."

The first thing I noticed after slipping into the interior of the cave was that the temperature had dropped significantly. That alone made the trek worth the effort. Kyle walked slowly in front of me, reminding me continually to watch my step as well as my head. I was having the best time.

"Hunter would hate this," I told him, almost before I even had the thought.

Kyle laughed. "Yeah. He's a good guy, but not one to get sweaty and dirty while tracking down a hidden treasure that may not even exist."

"I'm glad we came. Whether we find the treasure or not. This has been an adventure of the very best kind."

Kyle paused and looked at the path ahead. "I've always dreamed of searching for buried treasure, but I don't want to get us lost. It looks like the path forks ahead."

I stood completely still. "What's that noise?"

Kyle hesitated. "It sounds like water. I think it's coming from the right."

"Let's mark this fork and head toward the sound of the water. If we come to another fork before we find the water, we'll just head back. I don't want to get lost either. We can always come back with better supplies."

Kyle left his hat at the fork so we'd know which one to take on the way back and then continued to the right. The sound of water got louder and louder as we walked along the narrow pathway. After a while Kyle stopped moving. "Why, I'll be."

I looked over Kyle's shoulder at a pool of water being fed by an underground waterfall. "Wow."

"Wow is right."

At the top of the waterfall, where the water entered the chamber from the surface above, there was a large hole that actually let in enough light to see fairly well without the flashlights.

The room opened as we continued forward. I dipped a hand into the water, which was fresh and cool. "This is really something."

"I could be wrong, but I'm beginning to think this map simply leads to someone's favorite swimming hole," Kyle said.

I sat down on the side of the pool and slipped off my dirty shoes and socks. I slid my feet into the water and let it pool around my knees. "After a long hike on a hot day this pool seems like a treasure to me."

Kyle removed his own shoes and socks and slipped his legs into the water as well. "Too bad we didn't bring swimsuits."

"I'm game for underwear swimming if you are."

"So am I." Kyle grinned.

I stripped down to my bra and underwear and slipped into the cool water. Talk about heaven on earth. Kyle slid into the water just after me and we both dove like puppies as we washed away the dirt and grime of the hike up the mountain. I swam over to the waterfall and slipped around behind it. I'd always wanted to view a waterfall from the back. Kyle swam around the other side of the waterfall and joined me. It was dark behind the water, which blocked the light from above. It felt like we were in our own little world.

Kyle turned and, without saying a word, pulled me into his arms. He leaned forward slightly and touched my lips ever so gently with his own. The kiss started off hesitantly, but in response, I imagine, to my enthusiasm, he deepened the kiss, and suddenly I was transported back to the dreams I'd been having all week.

There was something about being alone in the dark with someone I'd been dreaming about that brought clarity to my thoughts. Over the past few days I'd tried to make sense of the myriad of emotions I'd been experiencing since Kyle had begun kissing me in the fantasy world of my dreams. My logical mind refused to see it, but it seemed that every dream, no matter where it started, ended in this very real moment when I knew in my heart that I wanted this man as more than just a friend.

KATHI DALEY

Kathi Daley lives with her husband, kids, grandkids, and Bernese mountain dogs in beautiful Lake Tahoe. When she isn't writing, she likes to read (preferably at the beach or by the fire), cook (preferably something with chocolate or cheese), and garden (planting and planning, not weeding). She also enjoys spending time in the water, hiking, biking, and snowshoeing. Kathi uses the mountain setting in which she lives, along with the animals (wild and domestic) that share her home, as inspiration for her five cozy mystery series: Zoe Donovan, Whales and Tails Island, Tj Jensen, Sand and Sea Hawaiian, and Seacliff High Teen.

The Tj Jensen Mystery Series
by Kathi Daley

PUMPKINS IN PARADISE (#1)
SNOWMEN IN PARADISE (#2)
BIKINIS IN PARADISE (#3)
CHRISTMAS IN PARADISE (#4)
PUPPIES IN PARADISE (#5)
HALLOWEEN IN PARADISE (#6)
TREASURE IN PARADISE (#7)
FIREWORKS IN PARADISE (#8)

Henery Press Mystery Books

And finally, before you go...
Here are a few other mysteries
you might enjoy:

CROPPED TO DEATH

Christina Freeburn

A Faith Hunter Scrap This Mystery (#1)

Former US Army JAG specialist, Faith Hunter, returns to her West Virginia home to work in her grandmothers' scrapbooking store determined to lead an unassuming life after her adventure abroad turned disaster. But her quiet life unravels when her friend is charged with murder—and Faith inadvertently supplied the evidence. So Faith decides to cut through the scrap and piece together what really happened.

With a sexy prosecutor, a determined homicide detective, a handful of sticky suspects and a crop contest gone bad, Faith quickly realizes if she's not careful, she'll be the next one cropped.

ARTIFACT

Gigi Pandian

A Jaya Jones Treasure Hunt Mystery (#1)

Historian Jaya Jones discovers the secrets of a lost Indian treasure may be hidden in a Scottish legend from the days of the British Raj. But she's not the only one on the trail...

From San Francisco to London to the Highlands of Scotland, Jaya must evade a shadowy stalker as she follows hints from the hastily scrawled note of her dead lover to a remote archaeological dig. Helping her decipher the cryptic clues are her magician best friend, a devastatingly handsome art historian with something to hide, and a charming archaeologist running for his life.

Made in the USA
Lexington, KY
25 March 2017